A Sugarloaf Valentine

ROSEMARY WHITTAKER

A Sugarloaf
Valentine

Rosemary Whittaker

Also by Rosemary Whittaker
> *A Sugarloaf Mix-Up*
> *A Sugarloaf Surprise*
> *A Sugarloaf Christmas*
> *A Sugarloaf Easter*
> *A Sugarloaf Secret*
> *A Sugarloaf Summer*
> *A Tale of Two Christmases*
> *A Boxful of Christmas*
> *The Christmas Cookie Club*
> *The Cinnamon Snail*
> *Sunshine State*
> *The Wattle Birds*
> *The Feijoa Tree*
> *The Villa Mimosa*
> *Making The Effort*

 Stopwatch Publications

First printing, 2023

ISBN-13: 978-1-922651-32-7

This book is a work of fiction. Names, characters, places, and incidents are the product of the author's imagination or are used fictitiously. Any resemblance to actual events, locales, or persons, living or dead, is coincidental.

Published by Rosemary Whittaker
www.rosemarywhittaker.com

Cover design by 100 Covers.

For the real Bernie, who is cuddly and delightful and would never dream of asking for a raspberry slice.

Chapter One

'And these are the cupcakes,' says Mr Mason. 'Cupcakes are an extremely important part of our business. Can you remember that, Lily, or should I write it down?'

I look at the cakes, wondering whether they contain some magical property of which I wasn't previously aware.

'Absolutely!' I say when it becomes obvious he's expecting an answer. 'Cupcakes!'

He doesn't seem convinced. 'We'll go over it all again after lunch.'

'I think I have it!' I say in alarm, but he's turned away to adjust the thickness of the bread slicer.

My new employer seems to have a poor opinion of me, although I'm not sure why. He only met me a few hours ago. He's entitled to form his own judgement, but he doesn't have much to go on.

I've correctly identified the names of all the cookies and cakes, mastered the complexities of the old-fashioned till, and even laughed at some of his jokes. I haven't commented on the ridiculous overall he's given me to wear, and I arrived at work this morning with my hair neatly tied back as instructed.

But he still seems pessimistic about my future in the baked goods sales environment. If I'd been anticipating a meteoric rise from shopgirl to store manager, his manner indicates I should lower my sights.

I'm not too bothered. This is a stopgap for a few months while I search for a job in my own field. I won't tell him that. It's better for him to think of me as a keen member of his flour-based product emporium, anxious for the honour of the bakery and deeply ambitious for my future within it.

I may never know what I've done to merit such pessimism. Mr Mason isn't the chattiest of employers. All I can do is radiate as much enthusiasm as possible and hope he revises his opinion of me.

He flips the sign on the door from *Open* to *Closed*. 'You have half an hour for lunch. Make sure you're back on time.'

I'm tempted to ask why a food-based business closes during what must be one of the best times to sell its products. I restrain myself. It's not my concern whether he makes a profit. I'm here to exchange sugar-filled treats for cold hard cash or the electronic version of it and to try not to misidentify the cupcakes.

Half an hour is an annoying length for a lunch break. There isn't enough time to walk home for some of Mum's leek and potato soup. She always makes it when it snows, and it's my favourite. She and Dad will soon be tucking into large portions of soup, with crusty bread and cheese from the local farm shop. I hope she's saved some for me.

There's plenty of bread available here. I've been too busy to think about being hungry until now, but the sight of the glossy loaves with their crisp crusts makes my stomach rumble.

'Are staff members allowed to eat the products for lunch?' I ask.

'You mean the cakes?' says Mr Mason.

'I mean the bread, although the cakes look good too. Not the cupcakes, of course!' I add, remembering his obvious attachment to them.

He frowns. 'Our products are for the customers, not the staff.'

'You mean I have to buy them?'

This appears to be a new concept to him. 'You aren't a customer.'

'But I could be,' I point out.

'Our products are for customers only,' he repeats.

I wonder what he would do if I came into the bakery on my day off, minus my fetching tabard, demanding to purchase an assortment of delicious cakes. Would I be treated as a customer or thrown out and put on some sort of list?

Even better, I could borrow Dad's balaclava and Ben's old combat trousers, burst in, hand Mr Mason a bag for life, and demand he fill it with as many vanilla slices and croissants as it will hold.

He tries to usher me out of the shop. He obviously doesn't consider me a fit and proper person to be left alone in such a tempting environment.

'Can you wait for a minute while I get my coat?' I say. 'It's cold outside.'

He gives an exasperated sigh, but I ignore him. It can't be part of The Sugarloaf Bakery's official policy to insist the staff risks hypothermia. There's a limit to the keenness I'm willing to demonstrate.

I zip up my jacket and pull on my knitted hat, and he locks the door behind us.

'Don't be late,' he says, and I suppress an urge to salute.

I watch him trudge off along the street. What am I supposed to do now? I could go to the Red Lion at the end of the high street. They have a roaring fire, and the landlord serves an excellent mulled wine in the winter. I regretfully decide against it. It might not create the right impression to turn up for my afternoon's labours smelling like a character from Charles Dickens.

I'll have to go home, after all. It's a ten-minute walk, so I can spend exactly ten minutes in the bosom of my loving family before facing the walk back. There will only be time for a coffee.

I set off in the same direction as my employer, feeling like the pageboy in Good King Wenceslas. Either Mr Mason's footprints don't possess the same magical quality as the King's or I'm treading in the wrong ones because my feet remain obstinately cold.

I walk briskly along the pavement, slowing down to negotiate the icier parts. I don't want a broken leg to end my fledgling career in the bakery business before it's even begun.

'Lily?' says Mum as I burst into the kitchen. 'I didn't expect to see you until this evening. Is everything all right?'

I collapse onto a chair. 'This is my lunch hour – lunch half hour, to be precise. Mr Mason didn't want to leave me alone in his precious shop, so I had to come home.'

'I'll have to get moving,' she says.

'Some coffee would be great if you have any.'

'There's some coffee in the pot,' she says. 'You can start with that while I make you a sandwich.'

'I thought you might have made soup,' I say, taking the mug she hands me and curling my frozen fingers around it.

'I was just about to,' she says. 'It's a pity you didn't tell me you were coming home, but I'll know tomorrow.'

I look at my watch. 'I have four minutes left.'

'Nonsense!' she says. 'Your father will take you back to work.'

She opens the kitchen door. 'Martin, start the car and get it warmed up! We'll need you in about ten minutes' time.'

'There's no need for Dad to go out in all this snow,' I say.

Mum looks affronted. 'Of course, there is. He *wants* to!'

I'm not convinced, but the offer of a lift is too good to turn down. Mum hands me a cheese and pickle sandwich, which I eat at top speed.

I finish my coffee in two gulps. 'Thanks, Mum. You're a lifesaver.'

Dad appears at the door. 'Are you ready, Lily? Your chariot awaits.'

I love my parents. They're always there when I need them, no questions asked. Neither of them has said a word about me losing my job in London last week. Instead, each of them called me to say I absolutely must come home.

They both made a different excuse. Mum said Dad's sciatica was playing up, and she needed some help in the garden. Dad said Mum has been a bit down recently and it would be a great favour if I would keep her company for a few weeks.

As far as I'm aware, Dad has never had sciatica. Also, the garden is currently under a foot of snow and absolutely no plants are visible. Dad's excuse was even worse. Mum has never been down in her life. She's the most relentlessly positive person I know. But I appreciated their joint effort to help me save face, so I agreed to come home while I looked around for a new job.

I arrived yesterday afternoon to be met by Mum's delighted announcement that she had secured me a temporary job at The Sugarloaf Bakery while I'm here.

'But you mustn't tell Mr Mason it's temporary,' she instructed me. 'He's looking for a full-time employee. He wants to train them from scratch.'

I felt guilty about getting the job under false pretences, but after a morning of being trained from scratch, that feeling is wearing off. I now feel I'm doing the workforce a huge favour by keeping this particular job off the market.

Mum hands me my woolly hat. 'Off you go, love. You don't want to be late back on your very first day.'

That's exactly what I want. I'd be delighted to be so late that Mr Mason has no choice but to fire me. But I need the money, and work around here is scarce. Also, it was lovely of Mum to rush around and find me a job before I even got home. I'll stick with it for now and do my best to live up to Mr Mason's exacting standards. Who knows, with diligence and application, I may one day reach the dizzy heights of employee of the month.

Chapter Two

Mr Mason returns from lunch in a better mood. I don't know what's changed. Maybe his wife had leek and potato soup waiting for him. Or maybe he's had time to appreciate the quality of the staff member who has so undeservedly fallen into his lap. Whatever it is, he greets me with a pleasant smile and hopes I enjoyed my break.

'Yes, thank you,' I say warily.

This change of mood might be a trap. He may be trying to catch me off guard before launching into an interrogation about the relative prices of eclairs and apple slices, with particular emphasis on the rules surrounding discounts for cream-based products after four thirty.

Perhaps he'll set me homework – a short essay on the difference between an Eccles cake and a Banbury cake. Extra points will be awarded for topological charts showing the relevant geographical areas of the country. Your work to be handed in tomorrow morning to your head of department. That would be Mr Mason. There are only two of us working here. I wonder whether this makes me the assistant manager, but I have too much sense to ask.

'Did you go home?' he asks.

Is there a binding rule in my terms of employment forbidding junior members of staff from straying more than fifty metres from the premises during business hours in case of an unexpected baked goods emergency? I must remember to check my contract.

He looks at me in mild surprise, perhaps wondering whether it was a mistake to employ someone who has trouble with the most basic of questions.

'Yes!' I say with enormous enthusiasm.

He looks even more surprised. 'I understand you are staying with your parents?'

'Yes!' I say again. I can't think what else to add.

'Your mother is a very nice woman,' he says.

'She really is.'

He takes off his coat and slips on a full-length apron bearing the slogan *Here to Serve*.

'She visited my wife in the hospital last year,' he says. 'Brenda was delighted to see her.'

I remember now that Mum volunteers each week as a hospital visitor.

'It was particularly helpful as I was away from home that week,' he says. 'My mother had a fall.'

'I'm sorry to hear that,' I say. 'I hope she's alright now.'

He lowers his voice to a respectful whisper. 'She's in a better place.'

'I'm so sorry,' I whisper back.

There's a long silence while he inspects a tray of oatmeal cookies. He looks up from them at last.

'Southampton,' he murmurs. 'I managed to get her into an excellent nursing home there.'

I'm not sure Southampton qualifies as a better place, but who am I to argue?

'Well,' he says more briskly, 'we can't stand around chatting all day. We have work to do before the afternoon rush begins.'

'What time does the rush usually start?' I ask.

'Any time now. Do you feel ready to serve an actual customer?'

We only had a few people in this morning, and Mr Mason insisted on serving them himself. He didn't want to risk losing his long-standing clientele by allowing me to sell them a sesame seed roll when they'd asked for poppy seed.

I pull on my tabard and prepare for battle. 'I'll do my best.'

'Remember the rules of customer service I taught you, and you won't go far wrong. Would you like to tell me what they are?'

I can think of few things I'd like less. But he's my boss, so I plaster on my most charming smile and rattle off the rules. Most of them are absolutely ridiculous, especially the one about we should greet and say goodbye to our customers, but I pretend to take them seriously.

'Very good,' he says when I've finished. 'Very good indeed.'

I'm not sure I like his amazed expression. A cynic might think it betrayed a lack of faith in my abilities as a purveyor of diabetes-inducing delicacies.

Before he can quiz me further on the complexities of the apricot as opposed to the apple slice, we're interrupted by the jangle of the doorbell. I instinctively straighten my shoulders as I turn to face the customer. My heart sinks when I realise it's Mum. What's she doing here? I'm not a kindergarten child taking part in her first nativity play. As far as I know, the wise men didn't bring doughnuts for the baby.

Her face lights up when she sees me. 'Hello, darling! How's it going?'

'Fine, thanks,' I mutter. 'What are you doing here?'

With any luck, she's here to announce a family member has been gruesomely dismembered in a freak accident, or the house has burned down, and I need to leave work immediately. This hope is shattered when she beams at me.

'I'm here for a cottage loaf. Your father and Ben finished off the last one with their soup. There'll be nothing to make toast with tomorrow if I don't buy more. Breakfast is the most important meal of the day, especially in this weather. You rushed out without eating anything this morning. That won't happen again, even if it means I have to get up at five a.m.'

Mr Mason looks puzzled. 'Why would you have to do that?'

'It's a figure of speech,' she says. 'It isn't so vital now Lily is working in a bakery.'

'Our products are for customers only,' I say helpfully.

Mr Mason has the grace to look a little embarrassed. 'That is usually the case. But you didn't tell me you had missed your breakfast.'

'It's because she was so keen not to be late on her first day,' says Mum.

I try to look like someone whose every waking thought is for the reputation and financial success of my chosen profession. I'm not sure I succeed.

'How is she getting on?' asks Mum, sounding like a proud parent hoping to be shown her daughter's finger painting of a Chelsea bun.

'Very nicely,' says Mr Mason. 'Lily has already mastered our basic range, and she has a good understanding of the till. She's picked it all up far more quickly than the last girl who worked here.'

I wonder how anyone could struggle with the names of a few pastries and remembering a few buttons. Still, it's nice to shine by comparison. And it may explain his less than welcoming attitude to me when I arrived.

'I'm sure you'll work very well together,' says Mum. 'Lily has always been a quick learner.'

'Not everyone is cut out for a career in retail,' he says. 'It can be very demanding.'

I barely manage to stop myself from rolling my eyes. I've spent the last year in London working as an office manager. But that's the peril of returning home. People see you as the child you used to be and treat you accordingly. At least, Mum does.

'I'm after a cottage loaf,' she says, scanning the racks behind me.

Mr Mason gives me an encouraging smile. 'Perhaps we should ask Lily to deal with that.'

I point to a loaf. 'I believe that's the one you usually have.'

'Perfect!' she says. 'You clever girl.'

I could have pointed to a currant bun and she'd have said the same thing. She's always been like this. She sees the best in everyone and encourages it. If there is no best, she sees it anyway, and somehow, it magically appears. I don't know how she does it.

I put the loaf in a paper bag and hand it to her.

'You're a pro already,' she says. 'Are you going to ring it up as well?'

I look at Mr Mason, who considers. 'I think you may be ready.'

I try not to giggle as I enter the price. I take the note Mum hands me and count out her change.

'Wonderful!' she says. 'I'll see you at home, darling. Have a lovely afternoon, Mr Mason.'

He actually escorts her to the door and gives what looks like a half bow as she leaves. I hope I'm not supposed to drop a curtsey each time anyone comes in. It wasn't part of my initial training.

The afternoon passes slowly, with no sign of the rush Mr Mason predicted. I wonder whether my presence has jinxed it. If so, I'll soon be out of a job.

He doesn't seem to notice anything amiss. He hovers over me as I serve the trickle of customers. His disapproving look gradually fades when he realises I probably won't plunge the bakery into bankruptcy on my first day.

I take a surreptitious look at my watch. Half past four. Only one more hour to go. It's already growing dark, and it's started to snow again. I'm not looking forward to my walk home, but I am looking forward to the end of my shift.

At five o'clock, Mr Mason instructs me to cover the trays of cookies.

'I doubt we'll sell any more of these today,' he says, 'but a few last-minute customers may pop in for a loaf of bread on their way home.'

The bell jangles, and he looks pleased. 'What did I say?'

I'm bending down covering the cookies with red checked cloths and don't look up. I've served everyone this afternoon. He can manage this one by himself. I finish the cookies and move on to the coconut slices. I'm about to ask Mr Mason whether we have any more covers when the customer speaks.

I freeze. I'd know that voice anywhere. I haven't heard it for nearly a year, but it's as familiar to me as my own heartbeat.

It can't be. It absolutely can't be. He isn't supposed to be anywhere near here. He's in Manchester. Mum told me all about his wonderful new job with Hewlett Packard when I was home for Christmas. I'm not sure how far Manchester is from Honeywell, but it definitely isn't commuting distance.

I keep my head down and concentrate on the coconut slices. It's vital they're covered correctly or something awful will happen to them. I forget what, but I learned all about it this morning.

I decide to stay down here until he's gone. It may not even be him. Lots of people have similar deep, gravelly voices.

'Lily?' says Mr Mason's voice. 'We have a customer.'

There's nothing for it. I slowly straighten up and find myself staring straight into Stephen Parker's eyes.

Chapter Three

For a moment, neither of us speaks, then his face breaks into a smile. 'Lily, it is you! What are you doing here?'

I stare at him, unable to formulate a coherent answer. I'm acutely aware of Mr Mason watching us. As far as he's concerned, Stephen is just another customer. My mind flips frantically through the list of directions for dealing with our clientele. None of the rules tell you how to greet a customer who appears without warning and reminds the staff member how completely they broke her heart a year ago.

'Hi, Stephen,' I begin.

I'm aware my voice is half an octave higher than usual. I lower it to a more appropriate level. 'I work here. What are you doing here?'

Mr Mason gives me a disapproving look.

I try again. 'I didn't know you were back in Honeywell. Mum mentioned you're living in Manchester now.'

'I'm home for a quick visit,' he says.

'To see your family?'

Mr Mason looks even more annoyed. I'm not sure why. I haven't asked anything personal. I merely enquired about the customer's family, which is a polite and appropriate thing to do. It falls under rule number four – inquire in a pleasant yet discreet manner about your customer's day. That's exactly what I've done. I haven't suggested Stephen's family is the lynchpin of the local drug trade or that they smuggle in exotic pets from the Far East.

Stephen gives me an awkward smile. 'Actually, I'm visiting my girlfriend.'

I feel as though he's thrown one of our extra dense wholegrain rolls at my head. This shouldn't be a surprise. We broke up a year ago. Of course, he's been seeing other people.

'That's nice,' I say in a strangled voice. 'Does she live locally?'

He shuffles his feet. 'She lives in Little Compton.'

'What's her name?'

'Isabella,' he says. 'Isabella Campbell.'

Mr Mason comes to my rescue. 'You and your friend must have a lot to catch up on, Lily, but we close in fifteen minutes. He may be in a hurry.'

Stephen clears his throat. 'I only came in to ask … but it was a stupid idea. I'll come back another time.'

'Not at all,' says Mr Mason courteously. 'We would love to help you in any way we can. Isn't that right, Lily?'

I hardly hear him. A flood of memories is washing over me, threatening to drown me. Stephen and me walking hand in hand along the riverbank. Stephen telling me I was the most beautiful woman he'd ever met. Stephen telling me he didn't want to see me anymore …

'Lily?' says Mr Mason.

I return to the present with a jolt. 'Oh, yes! What Mr Mason said.'

Stephen grins. He knows perfectly well I haven't been listening. I only hope he doesn't realise why.

'I popped in to see whether you might do me a box of cookies next week,' he says. 'It's Valentine's Day, and I thought it might be a nice gesture …'

He trails off, looking embarrassed.

'We'd be only too happy to help,' says Mr Mason. 'We have a fine selection from which to choose.'

Stephen glances at me, then away again. 'I was hoping to personalise them.'

'In what way?' says Mr Mason.

Stephen looks even more embarrassed. 'Could you ice some letters on them or something?'

Mr Mason looks baffled. 'What sort of letters?'

I can't stand any more of this. Usually, I'm all for watching a vaudeville act, particularly if it means I don't have to work. But this one is getting painful.

'I imagine Stephen means the letters of his girlfriend's name,' I say.

Stephen looks relieved. 'Something like that. Or some sort of message.'

I can think of several messages I'd like to ice on the cookies, but none that wouldn't result in my instant dismissal.

'This is my first day,' I tell Stephen. 'I don't know whether we offer this service.'

Mr Mason is wearing the look of a dog whose toy bone has been hidden from him. He knows it's somewhere, but he's not sure where to start.

'Is this a service we offer?' I prompt him.

'I've never been asked that before,' he says. His eye falls on me, and his face clears. 'I'm sure Lily would love to oblige.'

Stephen looks horrified. 'I wouldn't dream of putting her to all that trouble.'

'No trouble at all,' says Mr Mason. 'She'll be delighted to help you in whatever way she can.'

'Delighted,' I echo feebly.

'Did you say Valentine's Day?' Mr Mason goes on. 'That's most fortuitous. Martha always delivers a batch of heart-shaped cookies on the thirteenth. I'll make a note to put some aside, and Lily can ice them however you like. It's a very good idea. We could offer them at other times of the year too – Christmas and Easter and ...'

Halloween, I think viciously. I could do wonders with a bag of bright red icing.

'What's the message?' I ask Stephen.

'Message?'

'I need to know what message you want on the cookies. Unless you'd prefer me to make up my own.'

I'm pleased to see his ears turn a delicate pink. He looks at his watch. 'You're about to close. I'll have a think about it and come back when I've decided.'

Mr Mason looks disappointed not to have secured the order and started laying the foundations for our amazing new service.

'I'll pop in again tomorrow,' says Stephen.

'We'll be ready and waiting,' I promise with a touch of malice in my tone.

He won't come back. When he walked in today, I thought for one ecstatic moment he must have heard I was home and rushed over to see me. But it's clear he had no idea I was here and would have avoided the place entirely if he had known. Besides, he has a girlfriend. And not just any girlfriend – a girlfriend for whom he has come home especially for Valentine's Day, and to whom he plans to present romantic cookies with a personalised message.

My stomach does a flip as I wonder what the message was supposed to be. It had better not be a proposal. Customer service is all well and good, but if Mr Mason thinks I'm going to ice an impassioned declaration of love onto his vile cookies, he's sorely mistaken. I'd sooner quit my job and stay unemployed for the rest of my life.

In the unlikely event Stephen does come back to the bakery, I should put some boundaries in place – things I am and am not prepared to write on the stupid heart-shaped cookies.

Have a very pleasant day would be acceptable.

Make me the happiest man in the world by agreeing to be my wife would not.

'Perhaps we should pack up for the evening,' says Mr Mason. 'I need to show Lily what to do. It's a complicated process.'

Stephen catches my eye and smiles. I almost smile back, but I manage to stop myself. He doesn't deserve a smile. Not only did he dump me and break my heart, but he didn't have the grace to stay single for a mere twelve months.

'See you tomorrow,' he says, and I nod. I won't be seeing him again, but it's best to preserve the polite fiction.

Mr Mason jerks his head imperceptibly towards the inspirational list of rules on the wall.

I sigh. This has been a long day, and it's gone from bad to worse. Still, I don't want to go home and tell Mum I couldn't handle this job for even one day. So, I grit my teeth and force a rictus grin.

'Thank you for visiting us at The Sugarloaf Bakery. I hope your experience was everything you hoped for.'

Chapter Four

My walk home takes longer than it did at lunchtime. For one thing, I'm not racing back to spend ten minutes with my family before returning to the bakery. For another, it's more difficult walking in the dark. The pavements have been cleared with varying degrees of proficiency. Most people have dug out a path to their gate and piled the snow in random heaps along the pavement. I have to use the torch on my phone to navigate my way around them. Otherwise, I might pitch headfirst into one of them and not be discovered until spring.

Mum is in the kitchen when I arrive home. She's stirring something on the stove. It smells delicious.

She greets me with a delighted smile. 'I was getting worried. I was about to send your father out to look for you.'

'I came as quickly as I could. We're supposed to close at half-past five, but Mr Mason insisted on teaching me to close up properly.'

She holds out a spoon. 'Taste that!'

I open my mouth automatically. 'It's scalding!'

'What did you expect?' she says. 'It came straight out of the pan. It's chicken chasseur. What do you think?'

I pour myself a glass of water and take a gulp. 'It's delicious, as long as you aren't serving it with bread. I won't be able to look another loaf in the eye for a long while.'

'I'm making mashed potatoes,' she says soothingly. 'You must be doing well if Mr Mason allowed you to close up the shop. He probably hopes you'll do it all by yourself soon and give him an afternoon off. He isn't getting any younger.'

She brightens. 'He may be looking for someone to take over from him when he retires.'

'Let's not get carried away,' I say. 'It was kind of you to get me the job, but it's strictly temporary.'

She looks disappointed. 'It would be lovely to have you living in the village permanently. Your father would be delighted.'

Mum and Dad always do this. They don't like to put pressure on me on their own account, so they project their own wishes onto the other one.

'I'm an office manager,' I say patiently. 'I need to be where the work is.'

She picks up the potato masher. 'I know. But we plan to make the most of it while you're here.'

I leave her pounding the potatoes and humming *Sweet Potato Pie* and go upstairs to clean up before dinner. My legs are aching, and my lower back feels as though someone has been kicking it at regular intervals throughout the day. I'd love to have a hot bath, but there isn't time.

Instead, I take a shower with Mum's familiar rose-scented soap. She's used it for as long as I can remember, and it always makes me feel safe and secure. I'm convinced the smell of the bakery has got into my pores, and I'm determined to wash it off. It's a pleasant enough smell, sugary and fruity with a hint of vanilla, but I'd prefer not to be a walking advert for Mr Mason's products.

I wander back to my bedroom and put on my pyjamas. It makes me feel even more like the child who used to live here, but I don't care. It's so lovely to be home. I've been battered by the events of the past week. Everyone knew layoffs were coming, but I thought I was doing so well. However, as my manager told me very kindly, last in, first out. She's promised me an excellent reference, so hopefully it won't be too long before I find a new job.

In the meantime, I'll enjoy being home. I know how lucky I am that Mum and Dad will always welcome me with open arms, no matter what. Not for the first time, I'm grateful to have such lovely parents. Even my brother Ben isn't too bad – in small doses.

He's also temporarily back home. In his case, it's because he's broken up with his girlfriend and moved out of the flat they rent. Mum told me last night she's sure they'll patch it up because they're both such wonderful people. Until then, it's lovely for her and Dad to have the whole family under one roof. I don't know what's going on between Ben and Mia, but if relentless positivity can get them back together, Mum will provide that in spades.

I haven't unpacked yet. Mum emptied the wardrobe for me, but there was no need. I've only brought one case. I didn't want to make things too easy for myself. If she had her way, I would move in permanently, and she would look after me exactly as she used to. It's a tempting prospect, but it isn't what I want. I need my own life, which means I have to find employment fairly quickly. But there's no harm in enjoying a few weeks at home in the meantime.

My bedroom hasn't changed at all since I was about thirteen. Dad and I spent an entire weekend painting it pink and carefully stencilling butterflies all over the walls. It stayed like that until I went to university. I expected my parents to change it at some point, but they haven't, either because they've been too busy or because they want me to feel I always have a place to which I can return.

Ben's bedroom is also untouched. It's a violent shade of purple with a black ceiling. He was going through his goth phase when it was decorated. I wonder how he feels about sleeping in it after spending two years in his and Mia's delicately minimalist flat. Perhaps it will encourage him to seek a reconciliation sooner rather than later.

I put on my fluffy dressing gown and wander downstairs to help Mum.

'You look lovely and comfortable,' she says when she sees me. 'Can you set the table? Ben's always home by six thirty, and Dad's doing something or other in the garage. Give him a call when you've finished.'

Ben arrives ten minutes later. 'How's life in the fast lane?' he asks me.

'Fine, thank you,' I say with dignity.

'She's already managing the till!' says Mum.

Ben raises an eyebrow. 'Maths was never your strong suit, Lily. I hope you haven't bankrupted the business.'

'I'll have you know I've served several customers in an exemplary manner,' I say. 'Mr Mason can't think what he'd do without me.'

I may be shading the truth slightly here, but Ben doesn't need to know that. I doubt he ever goes into the Sugarloaf.

Dad comes in, and we sit down to dinner.

'An extra-large helping for Lily,' says Mum, handing me a plate. 'New jobs are always exhausting.'

'How did it go this afternoon?' asks Dad. 'Your mother says you're picking it up remarkably quickly.'

I ignore Ben's sardonic smile. 'It isn't exactly rocket science. I unload the boxes when they're delivered, and I put everything on the correct shelves. I serve the customers and give them their change. And I cover the cakes with cloths at the end of the day.'

'Richard Branson would be proud,' says Ben. 'Leave some mashed potato for the rest of us.'

'There's plenty more in the pan,' says Mum. 'Let your sister have as much as she needs.'

'Do you make all your bread on site?' Dad asks me.

'We don't make any of it,' I say. 'I don't know why. There's a huge kitchen behind the bakery, but Mr Mason has everything delivered.'

'He used to make a lot of his own bread and cakes,' says Mum. 'The bakery was quite a thriving business until a year or two ago. But he's approaching retirement, and I think it's become too much for him. He doesn't have many customers these days. I often wonder how long the bakery will stay open.'

It isn't until we're eating crumble and custard that I mention Stephen's name. Mum's bound to know what he's up to. She probably also knows this Isabella woman.

'The other reason I was late back this evening was because Stephen Parker came in as we were closing,' I say, without looking up from my bowl.

There's a pause before Mum answers. 'I heard he was home. His father's been in the hospital recently. The family has been quite worried about him.'

I hear the note of concern in her voice, but I'm determined not to betray myself. It was bad enough when Stephen and I broke up. I stayed in bed for an entire week, only emerging for meals. Mum was wonderful, but I know how stressful she found the whole thing. I don't want her to start worrying about me again.

'He told me he was here to see his new girlfriend,' I say in a casual tone.

There's a collective intake of breath around the table. Dad quickly covers it with a cough.

Mum lays a hand on mine. 'I'm so sorry, Lily.'

'Don't be! She sounds very nice.'

She gives me a doubtful look. 'That's good. Did you and Stephen have a pleasant chat?'

I consider how best to answer this. I suppose our interaction fell under the umbrella of pleasant chats. At least, I didn't launch myself over the counter at him and push his face into the mini pavlovas.

'That's right,' I say.

'What's his girlfriend's name?' asks Ben.

I pretend to search my memory. 'Irene, is it? Iris? I can't quite remember.'

'What does she do?' he asks.

'I'm not sure.'

'Where does she live?' asks Dad.

'Somewhere around here,' I say.

'How long have they been together?' asks Mum.

'I don't know.'

Ben helps himself to the last of the crumble. 'It's been great learning about Irene, or maybe Iris. I almost feel as though I know her.'

There's a knock at the front door, and I jump up in relief. 'I'll get it!'

'Who can it be at this time?' says Mum.

It doesn't matter when the knock comes. She always says the exact same thing. I've never known the time at which she thinks it's appropriate for someone to arrive on the doorstep.

'It's probably someone collecting for something,' says Dad. This is his invariable answer to her comment, although I can't remember anyone ever turning up on our doorstep waving a charity tin.

I hope it isn't Mr Mason, come to tell me I've forgotten some crucial part of the closing-up process and must return to the bakery at once to rectify it.

The knock comes again. It couldn't be ... of course not. But it's faintly possible. He knows where I live.

I open the door a crack and peer out. The figure on the doorstep is too tall to be Mr Mason, but not tall enough to be Stephen.

'Aren't you going to let me in?' says a familiar voice.

I fling open the door to see my friend Jack smiling at me. I throw my arms around him and give him an enormous hug. 'I thought you were collecting for something!'

He looks puzzled. 'Anything in particular?'

'Oh, you know. Charity, or a new sewage plant for the village.'

'Now we've established I'm not after your money, will you let me in?' he asks plaintively.

'Of course! I'm so pleased to see you. I was going to call you this weekend.'

I usher him into the hall and take his coat. 'Come on through. We're finishing dinner.'

He follows me into the kitchen. 'Hello, Ben. Hello, Mr and Mrs Carson.'

Mum jumps up to hug him. 'Jack, how lovely! Sit down, and I'll find you something to eat. Ben, put that spoon down right now! Jack wants some crumble.'

'I'm fine, thanks,' says Jack. 'I had dinner before I came here. My mother called to let me know Ben and Lily were both home. It seemed too good an opportunity to miss, so I thought I'd drop around to see them before they disappeared again.'

'I'll make us all some coffee,' says Dad. 'You young ones go through and make yourself comfortable. You must want to catch up with all the news.'

'Ben and I should clean up first,' I say.

Mum flaps her hands at me. 'Your father and I will do all that. Off you go!'

She shoos us into the living room like a mother hen directing her disorganised chicks.

'I think I left something in my car,' says Ben. 'I'll be back in a minute.'

He disappears, leaving me alone with Jack.

'It's so nice to see you,' I say. 'It must be nearly six months since we last met.'

'About that,' he says. 'I keep meaning to get up to London, but time gets away from me. I hoped to see you at Christmas, but my parents booked us all into a huge house in Cornwall. Amy and Mike were there with the children, which kept us all busy.'

He gives me a sympathetic look. 'I heard about your job. I'm sorry.'

'That was quick. Who told you?'

'Your mum told Mr Dobinson, who told his wife, who told my mum. You know how it is.'

'I do indeed. It's the worst of a place this size. No one's business is ever private.'

'It's also the best of a place this size,' he says. 'You're never alone.'

'I suppose you've heard where I'm working?'

'The Sugarloaf, isn't it?' he says.

'That's the place. I get to wear a hideous flowered tabard and curtsey to all the customers.'

His eyes widen. 'This I must see! Standards have obviously gone up since I was last in there.'

'I'm doing my best to drag them down,' I assure him.

I wonder whether to mention Stephen's visit but decide against it. There's no point. Jack must be absolutely fed up with talking about Stephen and our breakup. He came to see me every day during that awful week. He told me terrible jokes and took me out for coffee and played endless games of snap, the only game I could manage. I'll always be grateful for that, but I don't want to put a strain on our friendship by starting it all again.

Dad brings in the coffee, and Jack and I chat with him and Mum for half an hour.

Ben comes in after a while. 'Sorry about that. I needed to make a phone call.'

I wonder whether he was calling Mia. I hope this isn't a permanent split. I like her far more than any of his previous girlfriends, but it's none of my business.

'It's been great seeing you all,' says Jack. 'I have an early start tomorrow, so I should get going.'

'So has Lily,' says Mum. 'I want her to have a proper breakfast before work.'

I walk Jack to the door.

'Are you free for lunch at the weekend?' he asks.

'That would be lovely. I'm not sure which day I'm working. I'll ask Mr Mason tomorrow. He can't make me work the entire weekend.'

'If he does, I'll disguise myself as a delivery driver and sneak you away on a pallet,' he promises.

He turns at the gate and waves. 'Call me!'

He sets off down the street with his familiar, loping stride. I watch until he's out of sight before closing the front door. Despite what Mum seems to think, working in a bakery is not my dream job. But now I have something to look forward to. Jack is one of my favourite people in the world. Just knowing he's around makes the prospect of the next few weeks far more bearable.

Chapter Five

I arrive at work early the next day. I don't want to give Mr Mason any cause for complaint.

He almost smiles when he sees me. 'Good morning, Lily. Ready for another busy day?'

'Absolutely,' I say. 'It was interesting to learn so much yesterday.'

He looks pleased. 'I'm glad to hear that. It isn't everyone who appreciates what goes into running a small to middle-sized business such as this.'

Middle-sized is stretching it a little. Honeywell is a village with fewer than one thousand inhabitants. The row of shops comprises a tiny barber that almost always seems to be closed, a corner shop that functions as both post office and mini supermarket, a newsagent, and this bakery. Our much-vaunted afternoon rush yesterday consisted of four customers. The first one came in to ask where the nearest bus stop was, the second was Mum, and the third asked if we had any day-old pound cake we were throwing out because she wanted to make a trifle.

The other customer was Stephen. He definitely won't come back as long as I'm here. I'll be home longer than he is, which means our already small-sized business will have its takings reduced even further.

Mr Mason keeps a close eye on me as I remove the tray cloths from the slices and unpack the pallets of bread and rolls.

He nods approvingly when I've finished. 'Would you like me to refresh your till training?'

'I think I'm fine,' I say. 'I'll let you know if I forget what the buttons do.'

The doorbell jangles, making me jump. It's a hideous noise, somewhere between a yodel and a strangled squawk. I'm hoping to persuade Mr Mason to change it for something more melodious. If I get a new job fairly quickly, I could present it to him as a parting gift to ease the pain of losing such a valuable member of staff.

A middle-aged woman comes in, wheeling a tartan shopping trolley. A small dog trots in behind her, and Mr Mason's eyes widen in horror.

'Shoo!' he exclaims, clapping his hands loudly.

'Don't speak to Bernard like that!' says the woman. 'He doesn't like it.'

Mr Mason looks even more horrified. 'Do you know this dog?'

The woman closes the door. 'Of course, I know him! You don't imagine a stray dog has wandered in off the street?'

Judging by the look on Mr Mason's face, this is exactly what he imagines.

I take a quick look at the second list he's stuck on the wall. This one details the rights and responsibilities of our valued customers. It begins with explaining the circumstances under which they may request a refund – all of which strictly preclude any sampling of the goods. It finishes with a stern sentence to the effect that abuse of the staff will not be tolerated, and the proprietor will not hesitate to call the authorities should any occur.

Somewhere in the middle of the list is a rule stating no animals of any kind are permitted in the bakery for reasons of hygiene. It should say dogs. What other animals are likely to be brought in by their doting owners, especially in weather like this, when all decent, god-fearing rabbits, parrots and boa constrictors are safely in their warm houses?

'I'm afraid we don't allow dogs on the premises,' I tell her.

She turns pink with annoyance. 'Why not?'

This wasn't part of my training. Mr Mason led me to believe that all rules are instantly and graciously accepted by our customers.

'This is a place where food is served, madam!' he says.

She doesn't flinch. 'Why do you think I'm here? I'm not posting a parcel.'

'The post office is two shops along,' I say helpfully.

She withers me with a glance. 'I'm perfectly aware where the post office is, young lady. It was a figure of speech.'

She points to a garishly iced doughnut. 'I'll take that one.'

I pick up the tongs, but Mr Mason forestalls me. 'Don't move, Lily!'

I stop obediently, holding the tongs poised midway between the counter and the doughnuts. This is quite exciting. Who would have thought there was scope for so much drama in a small to mid-sized bakery?

'What are you waiting for?' snaps the woman. 'I don't have all day.'

Mr Mason has regained his composure. 'As I said before, it is impossible for us to serve food with an animal on the premises. I could lose my licence.'

She snorts. 'Listen to you! What are you – Harrods?'

He stands his ground. 'No, madam, I am the proprietor of The Sugarloaf Bakery. As such, I must refuse to allow any but service animals into the bakery on the grounds of hygiene.'

She wavers, obviously torn between wanting to storm out and wanting to buy the bright pink doughnut.

'He had a bath last night,' she says, but I can tell she's giving way.

Mr Mason assumes the stance of Custer at Little Bighorn. 'I must insist,' he tells her.

'But Bernard hasn't had time to choose his cake,' she says.

I turn my involuntary snort of laughter into a cough. 'Isn't the doughnut for him?'

She gives me a withering look. 'Not at all. He doesn't like strawberry.'

'What flavour does he like?'

She glances at the cakes. 'He's very fond of raspberry slices. They don't contain chocolate, do they? Dogs can't eat chocolate.'

I doubt our raspberry slice is on any list of canine nutritious snacks. However, Mr Mason is turning an alarming shade of purple, so it's probably time to bring this to a close.

'There's no chocolate in these,' I assure her. 'But should he be eating cakes at all?'

She gives me a withering look. 'Please don't tell me how to look after my dog. I only give him a small piece.'

'Fine,' I say. 'Are you paying by cash or card?'

'Cash,' she says suspiciously.

'That's fine. If you take Freddy outside, I'll bring your cakes out along with your change.'

She hesitates, considering whether I'm likely to snatch her money and lock the bakery door. She decides to take the risk. She hands me a five-pound note and takes Bernard outside, where the pair of them peer at me suspiciously through the glass while I ring through the sale.

I carry the bag of pastries out to her and wait while she scrutinises the receipt and carefully counts the change to make sure I haven't pulled a fast one. She nods curtly and sets off down the street in the direction of the barbers. Maybe Freddy is due for a haircut and a shave.

I go inside, where I'm pleased to see Mr Mason's face has returned to its usual colour.

'Lily, you were wonderful!' he exclaims.

'Thank you,' I say.

'I mean it! If I allow one customer to break the rules, it's the thin end of the wedge. It never occurred to me to serve her outside. When I next see your mother, I will make sure to mention what an aptitude you've shown for the business.'

I'm not sure whether to be amused or offended. Serving a cantankerous woman with a couple of cakes hardly makes me the bakery equivalent of Lee Iacocca. Also, I'm a little old to have my every move relayed to my parents. Still, I won't be here for long, and it's nice he seems so pleased.

A few more customers trickle in over the next two hours. Mr Mason doesn't attempt to serve them. He leaves it all to me. After my triumph with Bernard's raspberry slice, I'm not surprised. If things continue at this pace, I'll be assistant manager by Easter.

It's a shame custom is so slow. I'd prefer to be kept busy while I'm here. It may not be the most scintillating of occupations, but I quickly grow bored with staring out of the window at the shoppers on the high street, very few of whom seem to notice we're here. They go from the newsagents to the corner shop without glancing into our window, where Mr Mason has tastefully arranged an eye-catching selection of French Fancies.

I look at my watch and realise it's only ten minutes until our lunch break. I've promised Mum I'll go home for lunch, but I hope it doesn't become a regular thing. It wouldn't be so bad in the spring and summer, but it's a miserable walk through the slush and ice at this time of year. And ten minutes in my parents' bright, warm kitchen is worse than not going at all. It's a tantalising glimpse into another world – a world full of fresh coffee and home-made soup and uncritical adoration. A world, in short, that I left behind me when I left childhood.

I don't really want to return there, but it's oddly tempting. Adulthood is all very well and good, but it's considerably more painful than childhood. It doesn't seem that way when things are going well, but when heartbreak hits, it's all too easy to look back with regret.

As if on cue, the door opens, and the cause of my biggest ever heartbreak appears. I wasn't expecting him to come within a million miles of the place today. I can't imagine why he's returned when he knows I'm working here. Are there no other bakeries within a short driving distance to which he can take his annoying custom?

He looks pleased to see me. 'Hi, Lily. Is now a good time?'

There's no appropriate answer to this. Now definitely isn't a good time, but that's because no time is a good time to see him. How does he not understand that?

Mr Mason is fussing around at the far end of the counter, removing the last of yesterday's chocolate muffins and refilling the tray. I don't dare to be rude to a customer in front of him. It's a pity Stephen hasn't tried to bring a dog in with him so I could throw him out. His family doesn't have one because his mother is allergic to almost everything, but he could easily have picked up a stray on his walk over here. It's yet more evidence of his general thoughtlessness.

'We're about to close for lunch,' I say. This isn't rudeness. It's the exact truth.

Stephen looks disappointed. 'I didn't know bakeries shut at lunchtime.'

'Ours does,' I say. 'What can I help you with?'

I expect him to say he wants a split pan loaf or some wholegrain rolls. It is lunchtime, after all. But, to my surprise, he returns to the subject of cookies. I thought he might have had the decency to stay away from them entirely, but he doesn't. He seems obsessed with them.

Does he even know his girlfriend likes cookies? She may have a severe wheat allergy or be diabetic and have forgotten to tell him. In a way, it could be a kindness on my part to ensure this ridiculous idea doesn't happen.

'I was actually hoping to talk to you, Lily,' he says hesitantly.

'About the cookies?'

He glances at Mr Mason. 'Not exactly.'

My heart skips a beat. Not exactly? Does that mean he no longer wants the cookies? There could be plenty of reasons for that apart from the health-related ones I've come up with. Isabella may have texted him to say she's run off with the master of the local fox hunt and never wants to see him again.

To be fair, I don't know for sure she's into fox hunting. But it seems a strong possibility in the sort of person who agrees to start dating someone who couldn't remain single for one short year after breaking up with the love of his life.

Also, she lives in the Manor House. I've never been inside it, but I've driven past plenty of times. It's a huge house set in its own grounds, with paddocks and horses and a duck pond. If her family can afford to live there, she can definitely buy her own cookies. There's no need for Stephen to waste his money.

My mind has been too full of gymkhanas and hunt balls to pay attention to what else Stephen might be saying. I give myself a mental shake and return to the subject at hand. 'You could come back after lunch.'

'I'm afraid I can't keep the shop open any longer,' says Mr Mason. 'I have somewhere I need to be. And staff members can't remain on the premises over the lunch period for health and safety reasons.'

These regulations must exist solely in his mind. What does he think I plan to do – run amok around the shelves of pastries, hurling cream doughnuts at the walls? After an early start and dealing with Bernard and his owner, I honestly don't have the energy.

'Can I buy you lunch at the pub?' Stephen asks abruptly.

I'm too startled to answer. It sounds as though what he has to say to me will take some time, which could be good or bad, depending on what it is.

'I only have half an hour,' I tell him.

'That's enough time for a sandwich and a drink,' he says. 'You need something to warm you up in this weather.'

'A coffee would be nice,' I say for Mr Mason's benefit. A triple brandy would be more warming, but I doubt he would approve.

Mr Mason shepherds us both outside, where he appears to wrestle with himself for a moment before speaking.

'You were here later than I expected last night, Lily. And it may take us longer than usual to close up tonight while you're learning the ropes. Perhaps you would like to take a slightly lengthier lunch break today in lieu.'

If Stephen wants to talk about our relationship and possibly discuss resuming it, I'd like to spend as long as possible with him. On the other hand, I have no intention of sitting there listening to him prattle on about horsey girl. Either way, the prospect of some flexibility around my future lunch breaks is too good to pass up.

'That's very kind of you, Mr Mason,' I say, rather touched at his suggestion.

'Shall we say forty-five minutes?' he says. 'Just for today, you understand?'

'I'll be here on time,' I promise.

'We should make a start,' says Stephen.

Mr Mason looks as though he's already regretting his generous offer, but that's too bad. I set off as quickly as possible in the direction of the pub before he can change his mind.

Chapter Six

It only takes us five minutes to reach the Red Lion. The pub is just as I remember it – all exposed beams and flagstones, with a huge roaring fire at the far end.

'Are you still drinking red wine?' Stephen asks me.

'I can't,' I say regretfully. 'Mr Mason wouldn't approve of me drinking at work.'

'You aren't at work right now,' he says. 'Besides, if he gave you an hour for lunch, like any halfway decent employer, it would all have left your system by the time you got back to the bakery.'

'I'd like a glass of mulled wine,' I decide. 'But make sure it's not too large.'

'Would you like a sandwich too? I can ask Ted to hurry it up.'

'That would be nice. Is there a menu somewhere?'

He pulls out his wallet. 'There's no time! You have to be back at the bakery, remember? I know what you like.'

He disappears into the crowd around the bar. I ought to feel annoyed. The days of men ordering for women and returning with a small port and lemon are long over. But it's nice to think he remembers my likes and dislikes, even after a year apart and with one or possibly several new girlfriends in between. I wonder whether he orders for Isabella, and if so, what she has. She probably eats nothing but game pie and roast pheasant washed down with champagne.

I've built up a fairly complete picture of her, which I'm sure is accurate. I know her type. I grew up with them. I didn't meet them at school because Ben and I took the bus each day to the comprehensive school in the next town. But I saw the Range Rovers setting off from our village each morning towards The Grange, an exclusive private school several miles in the other direction. It's a boarding school, but it takes day pupils too. I expect Isabella went there. I bet she was Head Girl. I can see her now, tall and lanky, giving her end-of-year speech in her Barbour and green wellies.

Stephen returns before I can flesh out this picture any further. He's carrying two plates, which he sets down on the table next to me. 'I'll go and get our drinks.'

I peel back the edge of the nearest sandwich. It's my favourite, Emmenthal and lettuce, and I see he's remembered to ask for extra pickles. My eyes sting. He knows me so well. Why did he throw it all away?

He reappears, carrying two glasses of mulled wine. 'Are you alright, Lily?'

I blink hard. 'I'm fine. It's just the effect of coming in from the cold and sitting by the warm fire.'

He takes a bite of his sandwich. 'It's awful out there. It took me a long time to get the car out this morning.'

'When are you going back to Manchester?' I ask.

Maybe he'll be snowed in and unable to leave the village. That may or may not be a good thing, depending on what he wants to talk about today. I allow my mind to drift off into rosy visions of him telling me what a hideous mistake this new relationship has been, and how he realises his future is with me and no one else.

If so, I'm prepared to ice the cookies as a farewell gift. *Goodbye, Isabella. Sorry it didn't work out. See you around.*

If finances are tight, he could go for *Ciao!* which would have the benefit of being both non-fattening and economical. It's also probably the sort of thing she says to all her horsey friends.

'I'm here until the sixteenth,' he says. 'You aren't eating your sandwich. Did I order the wrong one?'

'Not at all. This is my favourite. You even remembered the extra pickles.'

He smiles. 'How could I forget your obsession with ordering pickles with everything?'

I take a bite. How was I to know he would remember? He's been happy enough to forget everything else. We haven't been in contact since that dreadful day he told me he couldn't see a future for us, so it was best for us to move on with our separate lives.

He's clearly done that, and so have I. At least, I've managed to get through each day, trying not to think about the fact he smashed my heart into tiny pieces with no warning. I've been mature and sensible and concentrated on working hard and advancing my career. I'd still be doing that if not for the downturn in the economy and my company having to tighten its belt.

It isn't my fault I've been forced to take a step backwards, living with my parents and working in a job I'll never grow to love. It's hardly your average thirty-year-old's dream, but I'm aware how lucky I am to have had something to fall back on. I wasn't the only one who was made redundant, and some of the other employees had families to support rather than an immediate offer of accommodation and as much home-made soup as they could manage.

Stephen breaks the silence. 'Are you sure you're ok?'

'Sorry, I was miles away. It's been a busy few days.'

'I can imagine. What brought you home? The last time I heard, you were living in London and working as an office manager.'

I take a slug of my mulled wine and almost choke. 'What do they put in this?'

Stephen tastes his. 'It's quite strong, isn't it? But you need it in this weather. It's antifreeze for your veins.'

I recklessly tip the rest of the wine down my throat. The worst Mr Mason can do is to fire me for drunkenness, which wouldn't break my heart. Speaking of broken hearts, I want to know what Stephen has to say to me.

'My company was downsizing,' I say, 'and I got caught in the crossfire. Is that what you wanted to talk to me about?'

'Not really,' he says. 'But I'm sorry it happened.'

'I'm sure I'll find something else soon.'

'Of course, you will. In the meantime, your parents must be enjoying having you home.'

'They are,' I say. 'It was Mum who got me this job. She's secretly hoping I'll discover a latent passion for retail and move here permanently.'

'Would you ever consider it?' he asks. 'You could apply to your old firm. I know they're small, but at least they're local.'

My heart skips a beat, and I choose my words carefully.

'I wouldn't rule anything out. I only took the job in London because it came up at a good time for me personally.'

I don't elaborate further. He knows exactly when I took the job and why. Anyway, he's moved away too, so that's irrelevant.

He finishes his mulled wine. 'I'm living in Manchester at the moment.'

'I know. Mum told me. I expect your mother told her.'

Silence hangs between us. Does he sense the unspoken implication that he should have told me himself? Probably not. Stephen has always been a practical person. When he makes a decision, he sticks to it. It would never have occurred to him to contact me and risk opening up the whole messy situation again.

'I only have ten minutes before I have to leave,' I say.

He shuffles his feet, looking like a small boy caught in mischief. 'I wanted to make sure you were ok.'

I don't know what he's asking. Does he mean ok with our breakup? It's a little late to ask me that. And he must know I'm unlikely to tell him the truth after all this time, especially as he appears to have moved on.

'I'm fine,' I say.

He looks relieved. 'That's good. It was horribly awkward when I came in yesterday, and I wanted to apologise.'

He leans forward and lowers his voice so the people at the next table can't hear. 'I couldn't stop thinking about it all evening. The look on your face when I told you about Isabella has been haunting me ever since.'

I stiffen. What look on my face? I'm pretty sure it only conveyed mild pleasure at seeing an old friend and polite inquiry as to the reason for his return to the village.

'I'm not sure what you mean,' I say. 'Did you think I was upset about something?'

'Well, yes. You looked pretty upset when I mentioned my new girlfriend. If I'd known you were in the village, and I'd be likely to bump into you, I'd have let you know. But I had no idea we were going to meet like that.'

I give him a cool stare. 'I may have been surprised to see you, but that's all. Why should I care that you're seeing someone else? You and I broke up a long time ago, and neither of us feels the slightest interest in the other one's life.'

'I wouldn't go that far,' he says, looking embarrassed.

I sweep on as though I haven't heard him. 'I'm happy you're seeing someone else. As a matter of fact, so am I.'

He looks surprised. 'I didn't know that. My mum passes on all the gossip from your mum, but she hasn't mentioned anything.'

I force myself to meet his eye. 'That's because my parents don't know yet.'

'That makes sense. I take it this is a new relationship?'

'Very new,' I say. 'But I think it could be extremely serious.'

He smiles. 'Despite being very new?'

I try to look dignified. 'It isn't all that new, but we haven't been together as long as you and I were. That's all I meant.'

He looks even more amused. 'I'm glad to hear it, or there would have been quite a bit of crossover.'

I'm starting to feel angry. It's insulting that he thinks I might be upset about his new girlfriend. It's even more insulting that he's brought me to the pub to persuade me to admit to it while he offers me sympathy. I don't need sympathy from Stephen Parker. I don't need sympathy from anyone.

'No crossover at all,' I say. 'But I started seeing him fairly soon after we broke up. It was casual at first, but now we're more serious. I expect I'll tell my parents about it while I'm here.'

'Did you meet him in London?' he asks.

My brother is quite correct to say I can't do maths, especially not in my head and while under pressure. How soon after breaking up with Stephen did I move away? And when did I say I met this man? My brain appears to have frozen.

'I met him the week before I left,' I say. 'He comes up to London quite often, and I see him whenever I'm down here.'

'So, he's a local,' he says. 'Do I know him?'

'I don't think so. In fact, I'm sure you don't.'

My head is spinning, although whether with the deception or the mulled wine, I'm not sure. I need to bring this conversation to an end before I dig myself in any deeper. All Stephen needs to know is that I couldn't care less about him or his stupid new relationship, and I'm blissfully happy in my wonderful new one.

'I have to go,' I say abruptly. 'Mr Mason will be upset if I'm late, especially after he's extended my lunchtime. Thanks for the sandwich. It was nice catching up with you. Maybe I'll see you around.'

He pushes back his chair. 'I'll walk with you. I'm going to the bakery, anyway.'

'You are?'

'I still have those cookies to order. I thought it would be a bit tactless if you were the one who had to ice them. But now I know you're fine ...'

'You can order anything you want,' I say. 'I'll be happy to help.'

We step outside, and I gasp as the freezing air burns a trail inside my lungs.

Stephen takes my arm. 'We should hurry. You only have three minutes. By the way, does this new man of yours have a name?'

My first instinct is to tell him to mind his own business. But that isn't what someone who is happily getting on with her own life would do.

'Yes, he does,' I say, almost tripping over a pile of snow by the gate.

He steadies me. 'I'm glad to hear it. It can be inconvenient going through life answering to, "Oi, you!" Are you planning to tell me what it is?'

A selection of names flashes through my mind. They race past so quickly that I'm unable to grab hold of one. Algernon, Cary, Albert, Marmaduke ... I wonder why my subconscious is throwing up characters from a black and white movie. Surely, I can think of one nice, age-appropriate name?

'Jack!' I say when the silence threatens to become embarrassing. I clear my throat and add more calmly, 'His name is Jack.'

'Jack,' he repeats. 'It's certainly better than, "Oi, you!" Well, I'm home for another ten days. I look forward to meeting him.'

Chapter Seven

Mr Mason is looking at his watch when I burst in. But I've made it with thirty seconds to spare, so he can't complain.

'I'm glad you came back to see us today,' he tells Stephen. 'I've been giving your request a lot of thought.'

Stephen looks taken aback, and I almost feel sorry for him. When he set out to procure his girlfriend a Valentine treat, he didn't have the faintest idea he would find himself enmeshed in a web consisting of his ex-girlfriend, her new 'boyfriend', and the possibility his request would lead to the entire overhaul of a long-established business. That's his problem. Everyone knows the theory of the butterfly's wing and the tsunami. It may teach him to think more carefully about his actions in the future.

Mr Mason pulls out a tatty notebook and opens it to a fresh page. He beams at Stephen. 'Perhaps you could give me some details about your girlfriend.'

Stephen looks at me, then away again. I have a fleeting impulse to help him out, but I squash it. I wouldn't mind hearing a few details about my rival. Not my rival – my unlucky successor.

Stephen fixes his gaze on a tray of meringues. 'Well ... er ... she's twenty-eight. She's about five foot eight and slim with beautiful curly hair. She likes horses ...'

I knew it! I said she was horsey. And true to shallow, predictable male form, he's gone for someone younger this time around. Only two years younger, admittedly, but it's the principle of the thing. It shows the direction in which he's heading. If he goes two years younger with each successive girlfriend, then by the time he's fifty he'll be giving Leonardo DiCaprio a run for his money.

The hair preference stings a little. As a child, I longed for curly hair. But my hair was ramrod straight and only got straighter as I grew up. Stephen always told me he preferred straight hair. Clearly, he was lying. All the time we were together, he was secretly wishing I was tall and thin with a mass of curls, and that I liked horses, instead of jumping in terror every time one of them makes that weird snorting noise.

I could fix two of the differences between me and his new girlfriend with the aid of a skilled hairdresser and a trained therapist, but the third is completely out of my grasp. I could never reach the dizzy heights of this Isabella stick insect woman, and there's no point trying. I've been shopping in the petite section of every store since the age of eighteen, when I finally accepted I must have been absent the day they handed out height genes.

I'd prefer not to hear any more. If we give him enough encouragement, Stephen may blurt out Isabella's bra size, and I'm not prepared for that.

'We only need to know what message Mr Parker would like us to ice on the cookies,' I tell Mr Mason.

'Quite so,' he says. 'Have you had any thoughts about that yet, Mr Parker?'

Stephen pulls a piece of paper from his pocket and smooths it out. 'I thought perhaps *Happy Valentine's Day Isabella.*'

He needed a piece of paper to remember that? It seems the kind of message which, with a little effort, he could have retained in his head until he'd put in the order. I wonder how long it took him to write it. Did he sit up for hours last night, chewing the stub of a pencil and trying out all the possible variations?

'That's a lot of cookies,' I point out. 'Twenty-six, in fact.'

Stephen counts the letters. 'You're right! Very impressive. How did you do that?'

I don't tell him that I too went through all the possible permutations of his likely message last night. He isn't known for his creativity, so this one seemed the most likely choice.

I shrug, trying to convey the impression of being some kind of maths genius – the Good Will Hunting of the bakery business. 'It's actually twenty-seven if you include the apostrophe.'

He narrows his eyes at me. 'We can leave out the punctuation for now.'

'That's up to you. You're the customer.'

'Quite right,' says Mr Mason approvingly. 'So, have we agreed on the wording?'

'Have we?' I ask Stephen.

He gives me an uncertain look. 'Now you mention it, twenty-six cookies *is* rather a lot.'

'Twenty-seven if we're preserving the punctuation,' I remind him.

He frowns. 'Perhaps it should be something a little shorter.'

'That's entirely up to you,' I say. 'We're here to provide a service.'

He looks at our display of cookies. 'How big will they be? Are the heart-shaped ones the same size as these, or are they more bite-size?'

Mr Mason considers. 'I believe our Valentine's cookies are similar to these.'

I'm starting to enjoy myself. 'Are we able to order custom sized cookies from our supplier?' I ask Mr Mason.

Stephen doesn't appear to think I'm taking this whole business seriously. 'There's no need to do that. I can make it shorter.'

'I don't mind phoning the supplier to find out,' I say. 'There's also the problem of packing them. We don't have any boxes large enough to lay out the cookies in a long message. It might be better if I put them into one of our regular cake boxes, all jumbled up. That way, your girlfriend could have fun deciphering the message before she eats them – like a type of edible crossword.'

'There's no need,' Stephen says shortly. 'Just give me eight cookies spelling her name.'

'Certainly,' I say with a professional smile. 'Are you sure her name is exactly eight letters long?'

He looks even more annoyed. 'Of course, I'm sure.'

I pretend to count on my fingers. 'That seems to be correct. And how are we spelling it? Is it the usual way, or is there a twist?'

His lips tighten. 'The usual way.'

'I thought there might be a *Z* instead of an *S*, or an extra *L*,' I say innocently.

Stephen turns to Mr Mason. 'I'll pick them up on the morning of the fourteenth if that suits you.'

He barely waits for Mr Mason's reply before turning and leaving the shop.

To my surprise, Mr Mason looks delighted. 'Very good, Lily! You handled that beautifully. It wouldn't have occurred to me to ask all those questions, but you're right. It's important to get the details correct, especially if we hope to add this service to our repertoire. I'll check that Martha plans to deliver enough cookies on the thirteenth. You can ice them when they arrive and box them up. If you can hold the fort for a minute, I'll call her now.'

He disappears into the back room, and I pull out my phone and text Jack. I don't dare call him because Mr Mason has oddly batlike hearing, and I can't think of a suitable excuse if he asks who I'm speaking to.

I can't say it's our bread suppliers. It may lead him to believe I'm planning to set up a rival guerrilla operation to poach his business, although I doubt that Honeywell is a prime location for pop-up stores. And all the other shop fronts on the high street are currently occupied, if not precisely thriving.

I decide not to give Jack too many details over the phone. Mr Mason is unlikely to have set up a staff messaging intercept, but it isn't a risk I'm willing to take. Besides, I don't know who might have access to Jack's phone. It would be easier to tell him in person. So, I send him a quick text. *Great to see you last night. Are we still on for lunch this weekend?*

I don't expect to hear back quickly. Like me, he's at work. But he replies almost at once. *Saturday or Sunday?*

I slip my phone into my pocket and gently knock on the office door.

Mr Mason peers out. 'Is there a problem?'

'I have a quick question.'

'Have you left a customer waiting in the shop?' he asks.

'No, and I'd hear the bell if anyone came in. I wanted to ask whether I'll be working this weekend.'

'Let me consult my rota,' he says.

He slides back inside the office and closes the door behind him. I wait outside, wondering what all the secrecy is about. It's an office. It isn't NASA mission control.

He emerges a minute later, holding a sheet of paper. He lays it on the counter and points to a carefully ruled chart. 'This is our staff rota. Do you see the title at the top?'

I suppress a smile. As an office manager in a large company, I had to produce spreadsheets showing the leave allocation for more than a thousand members of staff in four different countries. But I try to remember this is as important to Mr Mason as those spreadsheets were to my employer.

Mum told me last night that he's owned this bakery for thirty years. He left school at sixteen and started working here, and he saved enough to buy the business when the previous owner retired. It's nice to see someone fulfilling a lifelong dream, even if it isn't one I fully understand.

We study the paper together. He's written our two names across the top. Down the left-hand side are the days of the week.

He peers at the chart. 'Ah, yes, we are both here on Saturday. It's one of our busiest days, and we can't afford to be understaffed.'

'Does that mean I'm free on Sunday?' I ask.

He points to the chart. 'As you can see, only I am working that day. The bakery opens at seven at the weekends, but we close at lunchtime on Sundays, so I handle that shift myself.'

My heart sinks at the thought of getting up at the crack of dawn on Saturday, but at least I'll have the whole of Sunday off. I check the chart again and see I'm not in on Wednesday. That should break up the week a little.

I wait until Mr Mason returns to his office before texting Jack again. *Working Saturday. Free Sunday.*

He replies almost at once. *Sounds good. I'll book us a table somewhere and send you the details.*

Lunch with Jack sounds great. It's been ages since we caught up, and I'm looking forward to it. There's the slight added complication that I've recently announced he's my boyfriend, and apparently we're very serious. But that can't be helped. Stephen didn't leave me with much choice.

I'm sure Jack will understand. At least, I hope he will. I don't allow myself to consider what will happen if he says no. The idea of having to tell Stephen I made a mistake, and I'm not actually seeing Jack, is too much to bear. I could try to persuade him he misunderstood what I said to him at the pub. What I meant was that Jack and I were starting a business together and were partners strictly in that sense.

It wouldn't work. Stephen isn't stupid. He would know I'd lied, and he'd know why. He would be horribly sympathetic and understanding, and I couldn't bear that. I'd prefer to pack up and return to London and take my chances of finding a new job when

I get there. Mum and Dad would be upset, but that would be better than the humiliation of Stephen's sympathy. Even worse, his amusement.

I decide to keep it as a backup plan if things go really wrong. With any luck, Jack won't make too much of a fuss, especially when I explain the circumstances. It's the sort of miniscule favour friends do for each other all the time. I'd do it for him if he asked me. Anyway, there's no point worrying about it now. I'll just have to wait until Sunday and see how he reacts.

Chapter Eight

I sleep until ten o'clock on Sunday morning, then go downstairs to see where everyone is. I wasn't going to bother with breakfast, but Mum insists.

'Now, Lily, what do we always say about breakfast?'

'It's the curse of the modern age?'

She clicks her tongue at me. 'It's the most important meal of the day. Everyone says so.'

'The cereal companies say so,' I tell her.

It's no good. She already has the pans out. 'Would you like a full English breakfast or something light, like porridge?'

Only Mum could describe porridge as a light breakfast, particularly the way she makes it, with plenty of brown sugar and cream.

'Could I have a partial English breakfast?' I say.

She looks confused. 'I don't know what that is.'

'Eggs, mushrooms and tomatoes without the other things. Think of it as an Isle of Wight breakfast – small, yet part of the entire country.'

She's even more puzzled. 'No bacon or sausages?'

'That's right.'

'But you'd like some of my fried bread?' she says. 'You always have that when I make you a cooked breakfast.'

I waver. Mum makes the best fried bread in the world – golden and crispy and the perfect foil for bacon and sausages.

I shake my head regretfully. 'Just scrambled eggs with tomatoes and mushrooms, please. Jack and I will be eating in a couple of hours, and I need to have an appetite.'

Mum seems relieved I'm not facing the peril of going for more than two hours without a meal.

'I'll make you some toast too, just in case,' she says. 'Toast isn't filling at all. You won't even notice you're eating it. I have some lovely Oxford marmalade in the larder.'

I know better than to offer to cook my own breakfast. Mum considers both her children to exist in some precarious universe where they can barely manage to feed themselves or wash their own clothes. She stopped worrying about Ben so much when he moved in with Mia, but now he's back under his parents' roof, she refuses to let him lift a finger. As far as I'm concerned, it's very bad for him. It's probably bad for me too, but there's nothing I can do about that.

I make the coffee while she scrambles the eggs. No one scrambles eggs as well as Mum. I've never been able to discover the secret of making them as light and fluffy as hers. I've asked her several times to teach me, but I suspect she deliberately leaves out some essential part of the process so she can continue her unbroken reign as Breakfast Queen.

She hands me a plate piled high with toast. 'This will keep you going.'

I take the smallest piece and spread butter on it. Even Mum's toast is perfect. It's hot and crunchy and never seems to get damp and tough, no matter how long it sits in the toast rack.

Ben appears in his dressing gown. 'Fantastic! I haven't missed breakfast.'

'Not at all,' says Mum. 'What can I get you? I have everything here for a proper cooked breakfast.'

'I'm fine with toast,' he says, helping himself to the largest piece and smothering it with butter.

'You can't just have that,' she says, distressed. 'You must have something warming on a day like this.'

Ben crams the toast into his mouth and reaches for another piece. 'If you absolutely insist.'

She tips an entire packet of sausages into the pan. 'Quite right. A growing boy can't exist on a couple of pieces of toast in the morning.'

'Ben is thirty-two,' I say. 'He probably stopped growing a while ago.'

He smirks at me. 'Just because you only made it to five foot two doesn't mean the rest of us did.'

'Lily is the perfect size,' says Mum soothingly. 'She takes after her Grandma Rose. She was petite, too. She doesn't want to be six feet tall like you, Ben.'

Actually, I wouldn't mind. It would be nice to see over people's heads in crowds and reach high shelves without a stepladder. The only advantage I've ever found from my height is fitting comfortably into aeroplane seats. As I only fly once every few years, it doesn't seem an adequate trade-off for everything else.

I spend so long thinking about this that I don't remember my lunch date with Jack until half an hour before he's due to arrive. I shouldn't call it a lunch date, not in light of the news I have to break to him. What should I call it instead – our lunch engagement? That's far worse. Why does the English language insist on attaching such romantic terms to the simple act of sharing roast beef and Yorkshire pudding?

I finally decide on lunch appointment. It has a detached, professional feel to it. I try not to think about my last lunch appointment. Marnie, my manager, insisted I order the most expensive items on the menu before telling me in a hushed tone the company no longer required my services.

Hopefully, Jack won't react in a similar way when I tell him what I've done. I couldn't bear to lose our friendship. I've known him ever since I started sixth form college at the age of sixteen. He and Ben were in the year above me, which meant I'd already seen him several times in passing. But I met him properly when I started college, and our somewhat unlikely friendship developed.

I was shy and lacking in confidence, whereas he was at the centre of everything that was going on. But somehow, we hit it off, and we've been friends ever since. We've seen each other through failed exams and failed relationships and excruciatingly awful jobs. We know the best and the worst about each other, and we still like to hang out. It's the best kind of friendship, and I wouldn't knowingly do anything to put it in jeopardy. I may have told Stephen the tiniest of white lies about the actual nature of our friendship, but I didn't plan to do it, so it doesn't really count.

I run upstairs to take a shower. I wash my hair, then wrap it in Mum's favourite primrose yellow towel. I stare at myself in my bedroom mirror, trying to imagine myself with a mass of curly hair. Would Stephen have stayed with me if my hair had been different? It seems unlikely, particularly if this was the look I'd chosen. I look like a demented poodle.

The doorbell rings, bringing me back to reality. I hastily switch on Mum's extra powerful hairdryer. It immediately turns my hair into candyfloss. I switch it from cyclone to gentle breeze and restore my hair to some semblance of order. Then I pull on a pair of jeans and my warmest sweater and run downstairs.

I find Jack in the kitchen, politely refusing the slice of toast Mum is doing her best to thrust into his hands.

'You don't know how long they'll keep you waiting for your table,' she says. 'Why not take it with you?'

We leave her staring forlornly at the piece of toast and wave goodbye to Dad, who's oiling the hinge on the garage door and showing no signs of sciatica.

Jack starts the car. 'I'm glad you appeared when you did, or your mum would have started force-feeding me leftovers. No one ever goes hungry in your house, do they? I used to love coming over for dinner when we were younger. She always insisted on giving me third helpings.'

I settle into my seat. 'As far as I remember, you never raised any objection.'

'I was a teenage boy,' he says. 'I needed to keep up my energy for being cool.'

'You were incredibly cool,' I admit. 'I remember you and Ben doing wheelies on your BMX bikes for the benefit of all the local girls. I can't think how any of them managed to resist.'

'It's a mystery, isn't it?' he agrees. 'I couldn't understand it then, and I can't understand it now.'

He swings the car off the main road and along a gravel drive and pulls up outside The Wild Horse. 'I hope you're hungry.'

I follow him towards the main entrance. 'I thought we'd be going to a pub. This place looks terribly upmarket. I'm not dressed for it.'

'I'm sure they'll lend you a jacket and tie if need be,' he says.

I stay two steps behind him as he approaches the front desk. 'Table for two. Name of Fisher.'

Thankfully, the man doesn't bat an eyelid at the sight of my old jeans and wild hair. He leads us across the vestibule and into a small dining room, where I'm thankful to see people wearing a variety of outfits.

Two elderly women in tweed suits and brogues are talking earnestly together over their soup, while a harassed looking couple is sitting in the corner with their two young children. The little girl is dressed as Red Riding Hood. The little boy has made an even more daring fashion choice. He's dressed head to toe in a Spider-Man suit, including the hood, but he's chosen to accessorise it with a pink tutu and sparkly tiara.

Jack gives him an approving look. 'That outfit could have missed the mark, but he's managed to make it work.'

The server shows us to a table by the window and hands us both a menu.

'This one's on me,' says Jack before I can speak.

'Don't be ridiculous,' I say. 'I haven't seen you for ages. I plan to get this one.'

'You can get the next one. I chose this place. I'm paying.'

'The thing is,' I tell him, 'there may not be a next one.'

His brow furrows. 'You aren't going back to London at once?'

'I don't think so. But I may have to.'

He closes his menu. 'Let's order, and you can tell me all about it.'

He orders a steak with fondant potatoes, while I choose the salmon. I love it, and Mum only rarely cooks it because Dad is allergic to fish.

'And to drink?' asks the server.

'I think we'll need some wine,' says Jack. 'What do you think, Lily?'

I force a smile. 'At the very least. You may need something stronger by the time the meal's finished.'

He doesn't look too bothered. 'Let's start with the wine and see how we go.'

Thankfully, the server returns almost immediately with our drinks. I down half of mine in one gulp, and Jack looks concerned.

'Has something happened, Lily? Your Mum didn't mention anything.'

'Nothing too awful,' I say. 'At least, I hope you'll agree. It's just something I've done that I wish I hadn't.'

'I'm intrigued,' he says. 'Do you want to tell me now or wait until the food arrives?'

I finish my wine, and he waves to the server and points to my glass.

'Why don't you tell me what it is and get it over with?' he says. 'You won't enjoy your dinner otherwise, and it would be a shame to waste a perfectly good piece of salmon.'

He's right. There's no sense in putting this off any longer. If he's going to be angry with me, I may as well find out now and pack my suitcase as soon as I get home.

I take a deep breath, trying to think where to start. 'You already know I came home because I lost my job.'

He nods. 'I imagine you were pretty upset about that.'

'I wasn't too thrilled, but these things happen. And I was lucky to have somewhere to go while I picked up the pieces.'

'True,' he says. 'Your parents are great.'

'They are. I know how fortunate I am. Mum got me the job in the bakery before I arrived home.'

'What's the problem?' he asks gently. 'Do you hate it that much?'

'I don't hate it at all. I'm not saying it's my dream job, but it's absolutely fine. Mr Mason is nice enough, and I'm not exactly rushed off my feet. We have very few customers.'

'So, what's the problem?' he prompts me again.

'The problem is one particular customer.'

He stops smiling. 'What do you mean? Is someone stalking you?'

'I'm talking about Stephen,' I say.

'Stephen's stalking you?'

'No, he isn't. But he came into the shop on my first afternoon and took me by surprise.'

'You didn't know he was home?' he says.

'No, I didn't. And he didn't know I was home or that I was working in the bakery. It was pretty awkward.'

'I imagine it was,' he says. 'But you were bound to bump into him sooner or later. You both have parents who live in the village, so it's inevitable you'll be home at the same time. Did you see him at Christmas?'

Our meals arrive, and I feel suddenly hungry. I take a forkful of salmon. 'This is really good. No, he wasn't home for Christmas. He went skiing or something.'

'I see. How long is he back for?'

I stab one of the new potatoes viciously with my fork. 'I'm not exactly sure. But he's come home for Valentine's Day.'

Jack looks up from his steak. 'He happens to be home over Valentine's Day, or he's come home for Valentine's Day?'

'The second one.' I roll my potato moodily through the dill sauce and stuff it into my mouth.

He gives me a sympathetic look. 'I think I know what's coming.'

I nod. 'Mum told me he was visiting his Dad. But Stephen said he was here to see his new girlfriend.'

'I suppose it was inevitable sometime,' he says. 'It's been a year.'

'We don't know he waited a year,' I say. 'For all I know, he may have started seeing this woman the day after he broke up with me.'

He takes a sip of his wine. 'That's possible. But I don't see what difference that makes, so long as he wasn't seeing her while he was with you. Once you'd broken up, you were both free agents.'

'I know that!' I say. 'I understand how relationships work.'

He doesn't react to my snippy tone. 'What's this really about? Is it that he's seeing someone new, or is something else going on?'

I stare out of the window, trying to compose myself. 'It was all such a shock. I knew he was bound to start seeing other people at some point. But I didn't count on him waltzing into my place of work and demanding I write stupid messages for her all over our heart-shaped cookies.'

His lips twitch, but to his credit, he doesn't laugh. He reaches over and gives my hand a sympathetic squeeze. 'I'm not sure anyone ever expects that. It's like the Spanish Inquisition.'

I smile. 'In Stephen's defence, he had no idea I was working there. He thought he'd be seeing Mr Mason.'

'I don't know Mr Mason very well,' says Jack, 'but he isn't my idea of Cupid. However, appearances are deceptive, and who are we to judge?'

'Mr Mason was terribly confused,' I say. 'You'd have thought Stephen had stormed in demanding we turned the bakery into a gambling den.'

'It's lucky you were there,' says Jack.

I stop laughing. 'I didn't feel lucky. I felt like tipping a box of cookies over Stephen's head.'

'So, what happened?'

I finish my salmon and push away my plate. 'You'll be proud to hear I acted like the true professional I am. I suggested that Stephen go away and think about the message he'd like to write. I wanted to get rid of him. I honestly didn't expect to see him again.'

Jack looks dumbfounded. 'Are you saying he came in a second time?'

'The very next day.'

'I was right in my first supposition,' he says. 'You do have a stalker. Would you like me to alert the authorities?'

'Not yet, but I'll let you know. I haven't told you the reason he came back. He asked me out to lunch because he wanted to talk to me.'

Jack gives me a quick look but doesn't say anything.

'At first, I thought … but it wasn't that.' My face burns with the remembrance of that humiliating lunch.

'You don't have to tell me,' he says.

'Actually, I do. It's more complicated than icing cookies.'

I sneak a look at him and see he's looking amused. 'I mean it, Jack. You won't be smiling by the time I've finished.'

The server arrives to take our plates. 'Would you like to see the dessert menu?'

Jack looks at my flushed face. 'Perhaps in a minute.'

I wait until the server has left before speaking again. 'Stephen wanted to talk to me because he thought I was really upset about this Irene woman.'

He raises an eyebrow. 'Irene?'

I don't have to pretend to Jack that I've forgotten her name. 'Sorry, her name is Isabella. Anyway, Stephen wanted to check I was ok about it all.'

'Which you weren't,' he interrupts, keeping his eyes fixed on me.

'But he had no right to assume that!' I say hotly. 'I don't know where he got the idea I was upset. I was extremely polite to him, and I agreed to ice the cookies. What else did he want me to do – offer to be Isabella's bridesmaid or act as godmother to their firstborn son?'

Jack looks startled. 'They're getting married?'

'No!' I must have spoken more loudly than I intended because several heads swivel to look at us. I give the Spider-Man ballerina a thumbs up before continuing.

'Of course, they aren't getting married. At least, he didn't mention it. All he wanted was a Valentine's Day present for her. He isn't the most imaginative person I know, so I'm surprised he managed to come up with the idea of cookies. The first year we were together, he gave me a book on databases for Valentine's Day because he knew I was struggling with my IT qualification.'

Jack makes a small sound. I decide to interpret it as a cough. 'How thoughtful of him,' he says.

'Wasn't it? I'd spent the previous three months knitting him this amazing Icelandic sweater because he really liked the ones on that Danish show. You can't imagine how bad I felt about my lack of effort when I received my romantic computing book.'

'What did he get you the following year?' he asks. 'A slide rule?'

'He booked us a mini break in the Lake District,' I admit.

'It's nice to know he's capable of learning from his mistakes.'

I don't answer. It was a lovely thought, and we had a great time. But he broke up with me a week later, so it obviously didn't mean as much to him as it did to me.

Jack senses my mood and changes the subject. 'You were talking about having lunch with him so he could check you were ok. That isn't too bad. It's not as though he told you he'd put his Icelandic sweater on eBay or had always hated your taste in shoes.'

'He may as well have done. He thought I was upset because he was seeing someone else. You can imagine how that felt.'

'I can,' he agrees. 'What did you say?'

'I told him he was completely wrong. I wasn't remotely upset. I told him we'd broken up a long time ago, and I never gave him a thought.'

'Good for you,' he says. 'I'm guessing he didn't believe you?'

There's no point avoiding the subject any longer. He has to know some time.

'He didn't seem convinced,' I say, 'which was extremely arrogant of him. He kept giving me sympathetic looks. Honestly, Jack, I couldn't bear it. I wanted him to know I was fine without him. So, I ...'

'You what?'

'I said he must have been mistaken about how I felt because I was seeing someone else too,' I say in a rush.

'Good for you!' he says.

'I'm glad you think so. But that wasn't all. He kept asking questions about my new boyfriend. I tried to change the subject, but it was no good.'

Jack looks delighted. 'Why am I never there when anything interesting is happening? Did you tell him you were dating a supermodel who moonlights as a professional boxer? Even better, a famous actor? Extra points if you said you were seeing one of the Hemsworth brothers!'

'I wish,' I say gloomily. 'But you know me. I can't think on my feet.'

'I'm disappointed. You made up some boring boyfriend instead?'

I give him a sideways glance. 'Not quite.'

His eyes are alight with laughter as he waits for the rest of the story. Time to wipe the smile off his face and possibly end our friendship for ever.

'Jack,' I say as calmly as possible, 'I told him it was you.'

Chapter Nine

There's a long silence. I don't dare look at him while he digests what I've just told him. I dig my fingernails into my palms and wait for the explosion. It comes at last, but it's an explosion of laughter rather than anger. It's a relief, but I can't help feeling offended that he finds the idea of dating me so funny.

He wipes his eyes at last. 'Please tell me you're joking!'

'I'm not joking at all,' I say rather huffily. 'Yours was the first name I could think of. I told you I wasn't any good at thinking on my feet.'

'I suppose I should be flattered,' he says.

'Not really. It was only because I'd seen you the previous evening.'

'It's lucky you didn't see Mr Mason,' he says.

Whatever reaction I'd expected, it wasn't this. I'd anticipated he might be angry, although not too angry, because that isn't him. He's one of the calmest people I know. He would have every right to feel annoyed at me for dragging him into my power game with Stephen. But I didn't expect him to find the whole thing so hilarious.

He grins at me. 'Sorry, Lily. You took me by surprise, that's all.'

I laugh in spite of myself. 'I took myself by surprise. It was out before I knew it. He was sitting there looking smug and trying to commiserate with me. I wanted to make him stop.'

'I can understand that,' he says. 'So, where does that leave me?'

'Nowhere,' I say, surprised. 'I needed to tell you in case you bumped into Stephen, but that's all. He'll be going back to Manchester soon. I'll probably never see him again.'

'Will you tell him we've broken up?' he asks after a moment.

'I won't need to. I've already told you he and I aren't in contact. I haven't heard from him since we broke up.'

'So, he'll think we're still dating?' he says.

'I hadn't thought about that. It doesn't really matter. The only person who's likely to mention anything about me is his mother, because she knows my mum.'

'What does your family think about this?' he asks.

'They don't know anything about it, and I intend it to stay that way. Can you imagine their reaction?'

He looks hurt. 'I'm not sure I like being kept a secret from your nearest and dearest. It makes me feel so used.'

'I didn't mean it like that!' I say. 'Oh, you're teasing me.'

'Possibly. So, this is solely between you and Stephen?'

He no longer looks amused. I don't really blame him. It's a stupid situation, and I had no right to drag him into it.

'He isn't likely to spread it around,' I say. 'He was never one to gossip, and he's made it clear my life is of no interest to him.'

I try to keep the bitterness out of my tone, but Jack isn't fooled.

'He probably thought it was for the best,' he says. 'It didn't end too happily, did it? He isn't stupid. He must have known you didn't want to break up. What would have been gained by him staying in contact with you? It would only have given you false hope.'

I glower at him. 'It wouldn't have given me anything of the kind. I'm absolutely fine about our breakup. It's simply common courtesy to stay in touch when you've been together for so long.'

'You're probably right,' he says. 'Anyway, there's no point going over it all again. Whether or not he ought to have stayed in touch, he didn't. And now he's seeing someone else, and he thinks you are too.'

His familiar look of devilment returns. 'Did you tell him it was me?'

'You're the only Jack I know.'

'You know that,' he says patiently. 'But does he? Shocking though it is for either of us to realise, I'm not the only Jack in the world. There are plenty of us about. Did you specifically say Jack Fisher?'

I try to remember. 'It was all a bit of a rush, but I'm fairly sure I only said his name was Jack.'

I suddenly realise what he's saying. 'How stupid of me! I've been worrying about telling you all week, but there was no need. I could be dating any old Jack. Why didn't I think of that before? You're off the hook.'

'What if I don't want to be off the hook?' he says.

'You must! I'm only sorry I dragged you into this. Let's forget about it now and order dessert.'

He lifts a hand. 'Of course, I want to be dragged into this. It sounds like fun. And I definitely don't want you dating 'any old Jack'. We know nothing about him. We certainly don't know his intentions. He could be after your money or your job at the bakery.'

'He's welcome to either of them,' I say. 'Fine, I'll pretend it's you if it makes you feel better. But it doesn't matter either way. I only said it to shut Stephen up, and I achieved my aim. He couldn't get out of the bakery fast enough as soon as he'd ordered his cookies. Speaking of cookies, I want to see the dessert menu.'

Jack waves to the server, who brings them over.

I study mine carefully. 'I ought to choose something we sell at work so I can make notes on how to improve our products. But I want the sticky toffee pudding or the caramel sundae. I'm not sure which. Do you have a coin I can flip?'

'No, and I wouldn't give it to you anyway,' says Jack. 'That's no way to make a decision. Choose the one you really want.'

'That's the point,' I say. 'I don't know which one I want. They both look good.'

'There's bound to be one you want more,' he insists. 'Close your eyes and think about something completely different.'

I close my eyes obediently and think about Stephen. I'd forgotten how handsome he is and what a devastatingly attractive smile he has.

Jack's voice interrupts me. 'Open your eyes, Lily. What would you like for dessert?'

'Caramel sundae,' I say without thinking. 'Oh!'

He gives me a smug look. 'That wasn't so difficult, was it?'

'It was. I hate decisions. But it seemed to work. Is that how you make all your choices?'

'Sometimes,' he says. 'I usually know what I want, so I don't have to think about it. But it's a useful tactic when I can't decide. The trick is to let your mind go completely blank before choosing.'

'You told me to think of something entirely different,' I say, hoping he won't ask me what I thought about.

'That works too,' he says. 'At least, for dessert. I wouldn't use this method for anything important.'

'Like which job to take or whether to start a new relationship?'

He looks surprised. 'Possibly the job thing if I was offered two equally good opportunities. But never the other one.'

He smiles at my puzzled expression. 'Love isn't a decision you make with the flip of a coin or by closing your eyes. You just know.'

He's right. I knew the moment I saw Stephen that this was the man I wanted to spend the rest of my life with. That's never changed. It probably never will. But I don't want to admit this to Jack. I've spent the past year telling myself Stephen was a huge mistake, and we were never meant to be, but I never really believed it. When it comes to love, the heart knows exactly what it wants. It's simply that in my case, it isn't allowed to have it. At least, not yet.

I didn't expect to bump into Stephen again. I didn't even want to. But a chain of circumstances over which I had no control brought me home. And he happened to come home at the same time. Not only that, but he also walked into the place where I work on my very first day. Surely, that must mean something. It can't be a coincidence.

For the first time since Stephen and I broke up, I feel a tiny flicker of hope. This may not be the end of our story. Isabella is a slight problem, but not necessarily a permanent one. She may be nothing more than a slight roadblock in the path of true love. She and Stephen may not even be exclusive. I should have asked him more about their relationship when we had lunch together, but I didn't want to. I was too focused on disabusing him of the impression I was still hung up on him.

Perhaps it was a mistake to tell him about Jack. It momentarily soothed my pride, but it may have put him off the idea of us getting back together.

'Somehow, I sense you're no longer with me,' says Jack. 'Do you still want that caramel sundae?'

I come back to the present and smile at him. 'Try to stop me! And thank you for my lesson on decision-making.'

'One caramel sundae, and one sticky toffee pudding, please,' he tells the server.

He catches my eye and bursts out laughing. 'You're wondering whether you should have chosen the sticky toffee pudding, aren't you?'

I want to deny it, but I can't. He knows me too well.

'Maybe a little,' I say. 'But you can't go through life changing your mind all the time. I'll stick with my first choice.'

'There's nothing wrong with trying new things,' he says.

'Does that mean you're going to let me have some of your sticky toffee pudding?'

He grins. 'I walked into that one, didn't I? Fine, we'll split them and compare notes.'

We spend the rest of the meal chatting about everything that's happened to us during the past six months. I discuss my job and my worries about finding a new one. It's difficult to talk to Mum and Dad about it because I know how much they worry. But it's familiar and comforting talking to Jack. We've been friends for so long that we've developed a kind of shorthand. We seem to have an instinctive feeling for what the other one is trying to say.

When at last we can eat no more, Jack pays the bill and collects our coats.

'What now?' he says. 'Should we go for an extremely long hike to walk off our meal?'

'We could do that,' I say. 'Or we could go to my house and spend the afternoon slumped on the sofa watching a movie.'

He closes his eyes and appears to go into a trance. He opens his eyes dramatically and looks at me. 'The second one! My goodness, it really does work. I had no idea which I was going to choose until the words were out of my mouth.'

It starts to snow as we drive home, and I give silent thanks for his decision. I'm barely even a fair-weather walker. The merest hint of bad weather always sends me scurrying inside.

He parks on the drive, and I jump out and make for the warmth of the house as quickly as possible. Before I reach the front door, Mum throws it open, beaming from ear to ear.

'You're back, at last!' she says. 'Ben's told us the news!'

'What news?' I say.

She flings her arms around me. 'Your father and I couldn't be more thrilled, Lily. It's absolutely wonderful!'

She lets me go and makes a dart towards Jack, enfolding him in an enormous hug.

'Welcome to the family!'

Chapter Ten

There's a stunned silence. Jack is the first one to break it. 'Thank you very much, Mrs Carson,' he says politely.

'No, not thank you very much!' I say. 'What are you talking about, Mum?'

She pats my head. 'Don't let's stand out here in the cold any longer. You'll catch your death. Come in, come in, both of you!'

She slips her arm around my waist and leads me into the house before I can make a break for it. I'm not sure what this is about. Whatever it is, it can't be good.

Jack follows us. I give him a frantic look of enquiry, and he flashes me a mischievous grin.

We find Dad sitting in the living room, reading the Sunday newspaper. He jumps to his feet when we arrive. 'Marvellous news! Your mother and I are delighted, Lily.'

He claps Jack on the back. 'Well done!'

I drop into an armchair. 'Would someone mind telling me what's going on?'

Mum points to the sofa. 'Lily, come and sit here with Jack.'

'Go and sit over there!' she tells Dad. 'And take your newspaper with you.'

He obediently picks up his paper and moves to the armchair facing mine.

Mum pats the sofa invitingly. 'You sit here, Lily. And you too, Jack. We want to hear all about it.'

Jack immediately places himself at one end of the sofa. 'Come and sit with me, Lily.'

'I'm perfectly fine here, thanks,' I say shortly.

Mum's behaving as though she knows about our so-called relationship. But that's absolutely impossible. I haven't said anything, and Jack has only just found out. Which only leaves Stephen, and I told him very clearly that Mum doesn't know.

Stephen couldn't possibly have told her. For one thing, he isn't a gossip. For another, she's been here ever since I left. She was making roast lamb for her and Dad, and she never leaves the kitchen for more than five minutes when she's doing a roast.

'Don't be silly, darling,' says Mum. 'You know I prefer the armchair. It's exactly the right shape for me.'

She never sits in this chair. She rarely sits down anyway, but she always says her legs are too short for it. Is she planning to announce she has sciatica too?

She hovers next to me until I give up and grumpily sit on the sofa, as far away from Jack as possible. It's only a two-seater, so I can't avoid him entirely.

Mum sits down and watches the pair of us closely. She seems to be expecting us to perform some sort of trick, with Jack as the ventriloquist and me as his puppet, grinning at everyone and talking about *gottles of gear*.

'That's much better,' she says. 'Now you can tell us all about it.'

She gives me a roguish smile. 'And while you're at it, perhaps you can tell me why we had to hear the news from Ben.'

What does Ben have to do with this? I have to be careful here. I don't want to blurt out the whole story of lying to Stephen, along with the reason why I did it, only to find that Mum is referring to something else entirely.

'What has Ben said?' I ask.

'Now, you mustn't be cross with your brother,' says Mum. 'He wasn't to know you'd been keeping everyone in the dark. Even your parents,' she adds severely.

This could go on for a while if she doesn't get to the point.

'What did he say?' I repeat.

She clasps her hands. 'He happened to bump into Stephen this afternoon, who told him about you and Jack. There's no need to be shy. I can't think why you didn't tell us yourself.'

'What about us?' I ask.

'That you're courting!' she says excitedly.

'Courting?' I say in a tone of disgust.

'That isn't what the young people call it nowadays, Alice,' says Dad. 'Sorry, Lily, I think your mother means stepping out together.'

I give a snort of laughter. Jack is quicker. 'Or wooing,' he says seriously.

Mum looks delighted. 'I haven't heard that one for a long time. It's nice to hear some of the old phrases coming back.'

'Like sick,' Dad chips in. 'When we were young, it meant being ill.'

Time to bring this conversation to a halt. I have no wish to discuss all the words my parents' generation find confusing.

'Jack and I are not courting,' I say firmly. 'Neither are we stepping out or wooing or spooning or parking or going steady.'

I turn to Jack for confirmation. He gives me a reproving look. 'Perhaps we no longer use that terminology, Lily, but I'm sure you understand what your parents are trying to say.'

'Yes, but –' I'm interrupted by the doorbell.

'Now, who can that be at this time?' says Mum.

'Probably someone collecting for something,' I say before Dad can speak. 'Why don't you go and see?'

She jumps up. 'I suppose I ought to. I'll only be a second.'

Dad jumps up too. 'I'll come with you, in case ...'

They leave the room, shutting the door carefully behind them. There's no time to ponder the end of Dad's sentence, although I'm intrigued. In case the unexpected caller does what – tries to recruit Mum into a cult? But there's no time to speculate. I need to speak to Jack before they return.

'What do you think you're doing?' I whisper. I don't dare raise my voice in case Mum hasn't answered the front door but has gone to get a glass to press against the wall.

Jack slips his arm around my shoulders. 'What do you mean?'

I return his arm to its proper place. 'Don't play dumb with me, Jack Fisher. You know exactly what I mean. Why didn't you tell them we aren't seeing each other?'

'You mean wooing,' he corrects me.

'Stop it! This isn't the time to play games.'

'I don't agree. It seems the perfect time to me,' he says.

'You can play it by yourself!' I snap. 'It's bad enough having to lie to Stephen. I'm not doing it to Mum and Dad too. Besides, there's no need.'

'I disagree,' he says calmly. 'Think about it, Lily. Your mum says that Stephen told Ben, which means the news is out. You can tell your parents the truth and swear them to secrecy, but you don't know who else Stephen might have told. He's probably mentioned it to his girlfriend, and she won't have seen the need to keep it to herself. This sort of news gets about. It's inevitable in a small village like Honeywell.'

'If anyone mentions it, we'll have to deny it,' I say.

'We can do that,' he says. 'But that means denying it to Stephen too. If you don't, he'll only hear about it from someone else, which makes it far weirder.'

I open my mouth to argue, then close it again. He's right. I was stupid to believe I could tell Stephen about my mythical romance and not expect it to spread any further. Especially in a place like Honeywell.

I've backed myself into a corner here. Either I deny it to no one, or I deny it to everyone, which includes Stephen. I couldn't bear that. He'd know I lied to him. What's worse, he'd know exactly why. It's the very thing I was trying to avoid when I told him the lie in the first place.

But if I don't want him to know the truth, I can't tell anyone else, which includes Mum and Dad. Mum would be absolutely unable to keep it to herself. She'd let it slip within the first twenty-four hours. I wonder whether there's a train to London this afternoon. That would be the simplest solution.

'What's it to be?' asks Jack. 'You need to make up your mind before your parents come back.'

I can't think what's keeping them. Even if, for the first time in our lives, it was a charity collector at the door, how long does it take to drop a couple of pound coins into the tin? Maybe it really is a cult trying to recruit Mum. Even now, a couple of smartly dressed young men may be handing her flowers and convincing her of the benefits of selling all her worldly possessions and going on the road with them.

The door opens a crack, and Dad clears his throat. 'Is it all right if we come in?'

'Of course, it is!' I say more loudly than I intended. 'This is your house.'

Maybe it won't be for much longer. At this very moment, Mum could be signing a deed of transferral. But they may as well enjoy it for as long as they can.

Dad opens the door more fully and gives us an embarrassed glance. What was he was expecting – me to be pulling on my sweater inside out, while Jack hastily buttoned his shirt?

Mum appears behind him. 'Everything all right?'

'Wonderful,' says Jack in a dreamy voice, and she looks delighted.

'Who was that?' I ask.

'It was Ben!' she says. 'He'd forgotten his front door key again. Honestly, that boy would forget his head if it wasn't screwed on.'

'Even that's a matter for debate,' I say waspishly.

She ignores me. 'He'll be down in a minute. I know he'll want to see you both.'

This feeling is very much not mutual, but there's no point in saying that to Mum. She would never believe it.

She and Dad sit down again and look at us expectantly.

'What?' I say.

'You were about to tell us why we were the last to find out,' Mum says. 'You surely didn't think we would disapprove?'

Now is the time to tell the truth and get it over with. It's the sensible thing to do. It's the adult thing to do. It's the right thing to do.

I take a deep breath. 'We were planning to tell you all about it while I was home. We just wanted to find the right time.'

Jack takes my hand. 'It isn't the sort of thing you announce any old how.'

'Quite so,' says Dad. 'The important thing is that you've found each other.'

'I don't believe I was lost,' I say.

'Well …' says Mum. She catches my eye and stops. 'This is all so exciting. Ben is thrilled too.'

'What's Ben thrilled about?' says a voice in the doorway.

'Here he is!' exclaims Mum. 'We're talking about Lily and Jack's news. Don't worry. It's all out in the open now. You were only the tiniest bit premature.'

'That explains a lot,' I mutter to Jack. 'I always thought he was dropped on his head as a baby.'

Ben drops onto the sofa between us. 'Room for a little one?'

'Get off!' I yell.

He looks concerned. 'Sorry, I forgot! You want to cuddle up to Jack.'

'No, I don't!' I catch Jack's eye. 'I mean, maybe later. Anyway, you can cuddle up to Jack for a while. I'm going to put the kettle on.'

'I'll come with you,' says Jack.

'Don't bother.' I make a dart for the door, but he's close behind me.

I wait until we're in the kitchen. 'Are you enjoying this?'

'I am, as a matter of fact.' He reaches out and tucks a strand of hair behind my ear. 'You have such beautiful hair, Lily. I couldn't take my eyes off it over lunch.'

I stare at him, dumbfounded, then see he's grinning.

I lower my voice to a throaty murmur. 'You must tell me what you use on your hair. I want to run my fingers through it and tear it right off your head.'

He gently touches my cheek. 'Your skin is so soft. It's like the old saddle of my BMX bike.'

I feel a bubble of laughter rising inside me. I can play this game as long as he can. I consider what else to compliment. I'm about to say something about his muscles but stop myself. He does actually have a very nice physique. If I comment on his body, he may get entirely the wrong idea.

'I've always admired your ears,' I say. 'They're a perfect shape – like a seashell.'

'What kind of a seashell?' he enquires.

'A clam?' I say wildly. 'Depending on what a clam actually looks like. I've only ever eaten them in chowder.'

'A clam?' he says with a look of disgust.

'Not a clam,' I correct myself. 'One of those twirly ones. Or an oyster. Yes, that's it, an oyster! Have you ever thought of having one of your ears pierced? I could give you a pearl to wear in it.'

'If that's what you want, I'll have it done tomorrow,' he promises. 'Anything for you, my darling.'

'Well, isn't this adorable?' says an amused voice. Jack and I spring apart as Ben walks into the kitchen.

'What are you doing here?' I say.

'I came to see why the kettle was taking so long to boil,' he says. 'I should have guessed. Time loses all meaning when you're in love.'

'Yes, it does,' I say defiantly.

'Adorable,' says Ben. 'Mum and Dad are delighted.'

'As I'm sure are you,' I say sweetly.

'How could you doubt it?' He hesitates. 'Just don't ...'

'Don't what?' I ask suspiciously.

'Oh, nothing. I wondered, that's all. Forget it.' He ruffles my hair and leaves the room.

'What was that about?' I ask Jack. 'Why was he being so weird?'

'No weirder than usual,' he says.

'True. And at least he didn't pull any of that, "How dare you date my sister?" nonsense.'

Jack pulls me towards him. 'Where were we when your brother so rudely interrupted us? I think we'd fully covered the all-round attractiveness of my ears. Shall I move on to your lips?'

'Absolutely not!' I say, releasing myself from his grip. 'You don't need to do this when other people aren't here. In fact, you barely need to do it when they are.'

'Spoilsport,' he complains. 'Well, if I have to put my wooing on hold for now, the least you can do is show me where your mum keeps the tea bags.'

Chapter Eleven

Jack refuses Mum's invitation to stay for dinner. 'I wish I could, but I promised my mum I would go over tonight to reprogram her TV. I don't know what she does to it.'

Mum looks disappointed. 'We were looking forward to having you here this evening and hearing all about how you and Lily got together.'

I almost choke when she says this. Since deciding to stick to my story about Jack, I haven't had an opportunity to talk to him and agree upon the finer points of our narrative. Left to himself, I dread to think what he would come up with. He combines an extremely fertile imagination with an over-developed sense of humour.

I'll have to keep a close eye on him over the next week. Once Stephen is safely in Manchester, we can abandon the pretence, which will be a relief.

I don't know how I'll handle telling my parents about our breakup. Mum will be devastated. Dad, too. I knew they both liked Jack, but I wasn't prepared for their wild excitement when they heard we were together.

I don't really understand it. It isn't as though they didn't like Stephen. It would have been surprising if they hadn't. There's absolutely nothing not to like – apart from his taste in women. One woman, I correct myself. He obviously showed excellent judgement when he chose me. I still don't know what was going on with him when he decided to call it a day with us, but it was an aberration, and one that could very easily be fixed.

I've inadvertently made things more difficult for myself by this charade with Jack. Stephen's a very decent guy. I never seriously suspected he cheated on me with Isabella. He isn't like that. He's scrupulously honest and kind and would never deliberately hurt anyone. When he broke up with me, it was because he thought it was the best thing for both of us. He was completely wrong as far as I was concerned, but he did what he believed was right.

It's a pity I moved to London almost straight afterwards. It might have been better to stay in the area for a while in case he changed his mind. As it was, I left him alone, and everyone knows that nature abhors a vacuum.

I wonder how quickly nature filled that particular one and with how many contenders. It's unlikely that Isabella is the first person he's dated since he and I broke up. I hope she knows that. There's nothing more tedious than someone who thinks they're the centre of someone else's universe, when in fact they're barely even a star at the outer edge of their solar system.

'Can we have a quick chat before you go?' I ask Jack in a low voice.

Mum overhears. 'How sweet! You remember young love, Martin? We couldn't bear to say goodnight to each other, could we? Don't mind us, you two. We'll make ourselves scarce. Come on, Martin, I need you to help me with something in the kitchen.'

She never allows Dad to help in the kitchen. She's convinced he'll burn the entire house to the ground if he attempts to make so much as a cup of tea. I have no idea why. Dad is perfectly capable of cooking for himself whenever she's away, and he appears to enjoy it. But Mum likes to have one part of the house to call her own, and in which to show off her expertise. There's nothing wrong with that, and it seems to work for them both.

In return, dad refuses to let her fix the sink when it gets blocked, and he wouldn't dream of asking her to change a tyre on their old Civic. I suspect Mum is equally capable of doing both these things, but I've given up trying to convince either of them of this.

To their credit, they insisted Ben and I learned to cook and run a house and perform basic DIY and car maintenance. It's simply that when either of us is home, they revert to treating us as young children again and doing everything for us. Ben doesn't seem to mind. I'd hate it on a long-term basis, but it's lovely for the odd week.

I wonder where Jack will fit into this set up. Will Mum see him as the teenage boy she used to know and force feed him cake and offer to mend his torn jeans after a spill from his BMX? Or will she treat him as an adult, as she did Stephen? To be fair, it would be difficult for anyone to treat Stephen as anything less than an adult, even Mum. He exudes grownup-ness. I can't imagine him as a child. His family moved to our village three years ago, so none of us met him until he was an adult.

Jack is nothing like Stephen in that way. He's transitioned to adult life perfectly capably, but he's retained his infectious sense of humour and refusal to allow life to get him down. I wonder what Stephen would think of him if they met properly. They bumped into each other a couple of times while Stephen and I were together, but Jack was working away quite a bit and I was completely taken up with my relationship.

Stephen would probably like Jack because there's nothing about him to dislike. He's fun, kind, smart, and great company. But when I try to imagine the pair of them being friends, my brain gets stuck. I'm not sure why.

Jack would be bound to love Stephen. Jack likes everyone until they give him a reason not to do so. The only negative thing he knows about Stephen is that he broke up with me, and Jack is far too reasonable to hold that against him. He was hugely supportive during that first awful week, but I don't remember him saying a bad word about Stephen, which was probably a good thing. For all he knew, the breakup was only temporary.

None of this is relevant, anyway. With any luck, they won't meet for the next ten days. After that, Stephen will be gone. I don't know whether I'm looking forward to it or dreading it. If he insists on sticking with the horrible Isabella, I'm looking forward to it. But if he shows any sign of regretting his rash choice, I'd prefer him to stick around for a while.

Which brings me to the problem of having told him I'm in a committed relationship. Stephen would never make a move on a woman who was seeing someone else, even if Isabella were suddenly to disappear off the face of the earth. That isn't likely, so I try to think of what else might happen to her. Maybe her horse will throw her, and she'll have to spend the next six months in traction. That's no good either. Stephen is far too noble to dump someone when they're cocooned in plaster from head to toe.

The best thing would be for her to meet someone else. She's bound to have lots of braying, horsey types from which to choose. She may even have been secretly in love with one of them since childhood, in which case it would be a kindness to hope she gets her very own happily ever after.

'Lily?' Jack's voice breaks into my reverie.

'What?' I say.

'You wanted to talk to me? Isn't that why your parents have so tactfully left the room?'

His eyes narrow. 'At least, that's what I thought. Are you actually intending to make out with me? Your parents would be delighted.'

'Don't be so ridiculous. I told you we only need to keep up the pretence when strictly necessary.'

'I know you did, but I wasn't sure how seriously you were taking your method acting.'

I laugh. 'Not that seriously.'

'I'm disappointed,' he says. 'What did you want to talk to me about? I have to leave soon. I promised Mum I'd be with her about half an hour ago, and she worries.'

'I thought we should get our story straight,' I say. 'How we met, and all that.'

'You were dissecting a tadpole in Mrs Cornwall's biology class,' he says soulfully. 'A shaft of sunlight came in through the laboratory window and lit up your face. I knew then my life would never be the same again.'

I can't help giggling. 'I didn't do biology in the sixth form. I gave it up when I left high school.'

He looks shocked. 'Are you sure? Then it must have been somebody else I fell instantly in love with.'

'Very likely. We don't have time to talk about this properly right now. Can we meet after work one day this week and sort out the details?'

'Good idea,' he says. 'In the meantime, we can talk on the phone and text each other constantly. I'll be counting the minutes until I see you.'

The door handle rattles, and I hear Dad clear his throat again.

'If that cough of his gets any worse, he ought to see a doctor,' says Jack. He runs a finger down my cheek.

'What are you doing?' I hiss.

'I told you,' he murmurs. 'Method acting.'

Dad puts his head around the door. 'I'm sorry. I thought you must have finished …'

'For now,' says Jack. 'I'll call you tonight, Lily.'

'Not if I call you first,' I say in a sickly voice.

Mum appears in the doorway. 'Your mother rang to ask if you're still with us, Jack? She says she was expecting you, and she's a bit worried.'

'I'm just leaving.' He hesitates. 'You didn't, by any chance, happen to mention …?'

Mum looks shocked. 'Of course not! You must be dying to tell her all about it when you see her.'

'Or not,' I say.

Mum looks surprised, and I hurry on. 'It's up to Jack when he wants to make this public. In the meantime, we'd both appreciate you not mentioning it to anyone.'

'I understand,' she says, slipping her arm through Dad's. 'It's a very precious period, that time between confessing your feelings to each other and sharing your joy with the whole world. I wouldn't do anything to jeopardise it.'

I hope she means this. Her natural inclination is to share absolutely everything with everyone she meets, which would be a disaster. I can warn Ben tonight. He isn't one to gossip, anyway. He may mention it to Mia if they're in contact, but she and I don't know any of the same people, so we should be safe. If anyone will be a problem, it's Mum, but there's nothing I can do about that.

Jack lets go of me. 'I'm afraid I have to tear myself away.'

'Like an Elastoplast,' I say.

'What a romantic image! Nice to see you again, Mr and Mrs Carson. I'll see you again soon.'

'Although you did tell me you had a very busy couple of weeks ahead,' I say in a warning tone.

He touches my cheek. 'I'm never too busy for priorities.'

'How lovely!' says Mum.

She accompanies him to the front door, chattering all the way about new relationships and young love and what she and Martin always used to say to each other. As soon as Jack has left, I slip upstairs. I don't want to face any more questions until we've had a chance to talk.

'Lily?' says Mum as I pass her. 'Don't you want to stay and chat?'

'I'm a bit tired,' I say.

As I round the bend of the stairs, I hear her say to Dad, 'She's probably gone upstairs to play some music. Don't you remember how she …?'

I close the bedroom door thankfully and throw myself onto my bed. It's exhausting having a fake boyfriend. I haven't had one before, but they seem to be far more tiring than the regular kind.

Jack, on the other hand, doesn't appear to find it exhausting at all. He seems to regard the whole thing as an amusement laid on especially for his benefit. That's fair enough. I'd prefer that to him being angry about the whole thing.

I should have known I could rely on him. He's never let me down yet, and I don't expect he ever will. If we get through this without it turning into a complete and utter disaster, I'll owe him a huge favour.

I close my eyes and stop thinking about Jack. The more important issue is Stephen. I managed to salvage my pride by telling him this lie, so he no longer feels sorry for me. But he's bound to consider me off-limits now, which is the last thing I want. If he discovers he isn't as committed to this new relationship as he thought, I need him to consider me as very much on limits. Or within limits, or something.

This will take careful planning. I have to find a way to show him I was being truthful about being in a relationship with Jack, while also demonstrating that I may have rushed into it too quickly, just as he may have done with Isabella. I can't make a play for him while I'm supposed to be with Jack. Even if I could, I wouldn't. Stephen has to make up his own mind about what he wants. If this new relationship turns out to be what he's looking for, there's nothing to be done about it. I'll have to accept the inevitable and return to London, after fake dumping Jack.

There's still a slim chance that Stephen regrets breaking up with me too hastily. In which case, it would be better for all parties concerned to find out the truth as soon as possible. Maybe Isabella and Jack would get along? I banish this thought as soon as it occurs to me. They definitely wouldn't. Jack has never gone for hunting, shooting, fishing types. He's too down-to-earth and has far too strong a sense of humour.

I'm not sure what his current type is. It's been a while since we've exchanged relationship news. I must remember to ask him when I see him this week. Anyway, I'm reasonably certain this Isabella won't fit the bill.

When Mum calls me for dinner an hour later, I still haven't decided how to handle things with Stephen. I'll have to steer a middle course between making him think I'm madly in love with Jack and making him think I'm a heartless woman who's using him as a toy.

Bur there's nothing more I can do until I see Jack again, so I head downstairs for Mum's macaroni cheese, hoping she and Dad haven't decided to bring out their wedding album for the five hundredth time.

Chapter Twelve

I'm not too thrilled at the idea of going into work on Monday morning. It's been lovely having a day off, even if it turned out to be slightly more stressful than I anticipated.

A hideous noise rouses me from my sleep. I sit up and stare around wildly. It can't be my alarm. That's set to a soothing melody, which starts quietly and gradually increases in volume until I switch it off.

Mum comes rushing into the bedroom. 'Are you all right, Lily?'

'What's going on?' I say. 'Is there a fire?'

'The smoke alarm would have gone off if there had been.' She makes a dart for my bedside table. 'It's your phone!'

She jabs at it ineffectually before handing it to me. 'You'll have to do it. It's a different model to mine.'

This is hardly surprising, as she insists on using an old Nokia pushbutton phone. Ben and I have tried to buy her a new one several times, but she always refuses.

'Why would I want one of those? This one works perfectly well whenever I need to make a phone call. Dad showed me how to send a text the other day, but it didn't go well. I won't be trying that again. It came out as gibberish, and goodness knows who received it. Dad tried to find out, but it hadn't gone to anyone in my address book. I'll stick with this one, thank you. It suits me fine. I know you and Ben love yours, but according to Dad, you could start a nuclear war with one of those things. I don't know how you cope with the stress!'

I switch off the alarm. 'Sorry about that. I hope it didn't wake you. I must have knocked the settings somehow.'

Ben puts his head around the door. 'Hardly the behaviour of a good guest.'

I glare at him. 'Did you download that chainsaw alarm onto my phone?'

'I thought you'd like it.' he says. 'The other one doesn't appear to wake you up properly. I lay there for ages on Saturday morning waiting for you to turn it off. Beethoven's all very well in his place, but not when I'm trying to have a lie in.'

I put on my dressing gown and follow him downstairs, plotting a hideous revenge. I wonder how much it would cost to buy a police siren alarm tone and install it on Ben's phone – preferably somewhere it wouldn't be immediately visible.

He gives me a cheery wave. 'Must get going. Some of us have proper jobs. See you tonight.'

Mum puts a plate of toast in front of me. 'He didn't mean that,' she says soothingly. 'Working in a bakery is a very important job. It's the heart of a village. At least, it was before the arrival of supermarkets, and it still is. Think of all the old folk who can't drive. They depend on the corner store and the post office and the bakery. They couldn't manage without you. You're performing an essential service.'

I tip almost half a pot of jam onto my toast. It's Ben's favourite, so I consider it my personal duty to deprive him of it. My ears are still ringing from that hideous alarm.

'If people don't drive, they can get their groceries delivered,' I say through a mouth full of toast.

Mum hands me a cup of coffee. 'I suppose so, but it isn't very personal. At least they can enjoy a chat while you serve them. You may be the only person they get to talk to all day.'

I feel sorry for anyone if I'm the only person they talk to. But I decide to adjust my attitude while I'm working at the Sugarloaf. I have to be there whether I like it or not, and it wouldn't harm me to spread a little cheer when required.

I smile to myself at the thought of becoming known as the village sunbeam. People will start coming from miles around, driving past a host of other bakeries to be served by the girl with the personal touch. I'll be a sort of Florence Nightingale of shop assistants. We may become so successful that Mr Mason can open up a chain across the country and put Starbucks out of business.

He could promote me to work in the head office, where I'd never have to look another jam doughnut in the face. I'd certainly never have to ice weird calligraphy letters onto romantically themed cookies.

By a natural progression of thought, I remember Stephen. I doubt he'll come into the bakery again after I annoyed him last week. He'll stay away until the morning of Valentine's Day. It's likely he'll ask someone else to collect his order for him. His mother, perhaps, although I hope not. I've always found her rather intimidating. She and Mum get on very well together, so she must have some good points, but she's always struck me as a less personable version of Stephen. It would be excruciatingly embarrassing if she came in demanding her son's ex-girlfriend hand over a gift for his new one.

I look at the calendar with sudden hope. Maybe Valentine's Day falls on a Wednesday or a Sunday this year. My heart sinks when I see it's on a Friday.

I finish my toast and drop the empty jam jar into the recycling before Mum realises she needs to buy some more.

I arrive outside the Sugarloaf at exactly the same time as Mr Mason.

'Good morning, Lily,' he greets me. 'Did you have a pleasant day off yesterday?'

'Very nice, thank you,' I say, hoping he won't ask me what I did. If he does, I'll say I had lunch with an old friend and hope he leaves it at that. I wonder how he would react if I came out with the story of breaking the news to Jack that he was now my serious, albeit temporary, boyfriend, followed by Ben blabbing the whole thing to Mum and Dad, and Mum practically starting to organise the wedding. I wouldn't be surprised if she appears later to order the cake.

Will Mr Mason make me ice it? If so, it won't be recognisable as a cake. I could pretend I've gone for a snow scene – our front garden after a week of snow, followed by a thaw, followed by another blizzard. I could have a figure representing Dad pulling the weeds if his sciatica has finally cleared up. And another of Mum at the garden gate chatting to all the passers-by. I could ice a message across the lawn – *Better luck next time, Isabella!*

Mr Mason gives me an odd look. 'Are you alright, Lily?'

'Fine, thanks.' I follow him into the shop and start to remove the tray cloths.

He watches me approvingly. 'You're really getting the hang of this.'

I mentally roll my eyes. How difficult do he and Mum think this job is? Put another way, just how incompetent do they think I am?

I remember in time my resolution to become the shining light of Honeywell and look out of the window, hoping to spot elderly shoppers I can entice into the store to enjoy my sparkling repartee. No one seems to be about, which is hardly surprising at nine o'clock on a Monday morning. I'd be in bed if I possibly could. It's bitterly cold, the snow has melted to a freezing slush, and there's a chill wind.

I wonder whether it's ever occurred to Mr Mason to offer to deliver. I may mention it to him later, although I don't want to overwhelm him. He's only recently got to grips with our new cookie decorating service.

The morning passes slowly. A few customers drift in and out. To my disappointment, none of them are elderly. But it's perfectly possible to be lonely at any age, so I do my best to engage them in meaningful discussion. Unfortunately, no one is in a chatty mood, and all my pleasantries about the British climate and the current exchange rate are wasted.

I feel a flicker of excitement around eleven thirty when I see Bernard the cavoodle walking along the street with his owner. I prepare myself for another standoff and reiteration of the food hygiene rules under which we operate, but the woman walks straight past the bakery, despite Bernard's frantic tugging at his lead. I hope his raspberry slice didn't disagree with him.

Only one more hour until lunchtime. I look around the bakery for something to do. I could rearrange the macaron display for the hundredth time, but there are only so many ways you can arrange coloured discs.

Yesterday, I arranged them by colour from dark to light. I was pleased with the result until an annoying customer came in and bought four of the light pink macarons we optimistically label as strawberry. They look like the bottles of penicillin Mum gave me when I suffered from tonsillitis as a child.

If the customer had ordered one of each flavour, it would have kept my display symmetrical. I thought of suggesting it, but Mr Mason was there, so I didn't dare.

I could arrange them into attractive shapes if I had the slightest skill at art. I've always fancied myself as one of those artistic baristas who make the most incredible shapes on your cappuccino foam. But I can barely manage to draw a recognisable stick person, let alone produce a highly detailed and instantly recognisable picture of the Mona Lisa meeting the Dalai Lama on a Ferris wheel.

Still, I'm bored enough to have a go. I pull on my disposable gloves and pick up a circular display tray. Ten minutes later, I've given up all thoughts of emulating Rembrandt and settled for a smiley face using two chocolate and six raspberry macarons. I hope no one comes in today and buys one of the chocolate ones or I may have turn it into a pirate.

The bell jangles, and I turn to greet the customer, hoping Bernard's owner has had a change of heart. I've been looking forward to mediating another standoff between her and Mr Mason. But it's a young woman with fair, curly hair peeking out from under the hood of an old and exceptionally battered duffle coat.

She greets me with a cheerful smile. 'It's freezing out there!'

'It's nice and warm in here,' I say. 'Welcome to The Sugarloaf Bakery. How can I help you?'

I realise a moment too late that I'm supposed to say, 'How may I help you?' It's one of Mr Mason's pet peeves. But unless this woman turns out to be the linguistics professor from the local university, I may still get the sale.

'I'm after a doughnut,' she says. 'Unless, by any chance, you sell coffee? I didn't get one this morning, and I'm desperate for some caffeine.'

'Sorry,' I say sympathetically. 'We don't sell any drinks. I'm the same. It takes at least two cups of coffee for my brain to kick into gear.'

She looks disappointed. 'Just the doughnut, then. The biggest one you have! If I can't have caffeine, I'll have to rely on carbs.'

I point to our selection. 'Those are the iced rings. Our filled doughnuts are in that tray. They're bigger, but they aren't iced.'

She considers the options. 'I'll take one of each.'

I slip the largest of the jam doughnuts into a bag and add the chocolate ring doughnut she indicates.

She reaches for her purse. 'Thanks. You're a life saver.'

She taps her card on the reader and takes an enormous bite of chocolate doughnut while she waits. 'This has to go through. I'm not returning these without a fight.'

'I'm not allowed to fight the customers,' I tell her. 'My boss made that extremely clear when I started last week. He's a stickler for rules.'

'Are you new here?' she asks.

'Not to the village itself. I grew up here, and I've worked in the area for years. I moved to London last year, but I lost my job and had to come home for a few weeks while I look for another one.'

I hand her the card, but she doesn't leave. She finishes the chocolate doughnut and pulls the jam doughnut from the bag. 'That must have been tough. I've always wanted to work in London, but our family business is here, so it hasn't been possible.'

'What's the business?' I ask, watching in fascination as she crams half the doughnut into her mouth without getting any jam on her face as I inevitably would. Clearly, this isn't her first rodeo.

'Farming,' she says indistinctly. 'My family's been doing it for generations. I mostly work in the office, doing the accounts, but I get called on occasionally to deliver the odd lamb when things are frantic. I quite enjoy it.'

She makes short work of the second half of the doughnut and wipes her mouth. 'That was absolutely delicious! I didn't have time for breakfast today, and I was starting to wilt.'

'You came to the right place,' I say. 'Can I get you anything else?'

'I'm fine, thanks. I'm meeting my boyfriend for lunch in a few minutes, so I should save some room. We're going to the Red Lion, and they make the best steak and kidney pudding for miles around.'

My respect for her increases. I can demolish doughnuts with the best of them, but I wouldn't be talking cheerfully about lunch straight afterwards. She may not have been in the office today. For all I know, she's been out since six a.m. pulling mangle wurzels from the frozen ground and rescuing cows from snow drifts, or whatever it is farmers spend their mornings doing.

She hands me the empty paper bag. 'Do you mind throwing this away? My boyfriend hates even the threat of crumbs in his precious car.'

I laugh. 'I used to date someone like that. I accidentally dropped a bag of salt and vinegar crisps on the floor once, then stood on it when I was getting out. I thought he was going to cry.'

She peers out at the street. 'Here he is. Right on time, as always. That's another of his pet hates – crumbs and unpunctuality.'

'My boyfriend was exactly the same,' I say. 'Perhaps the two things go together. Does he also …?'

My voice trails off as I catch sight of the car pulling up to the kerb. Surely, there can't be two bright yellow Mazdas in Honeywell. That would be too much of a coincidence.

I take an automatic step back, although there's no need. The driver can't see into the shop from where he's parked. Our tasteful display of rainbow-coloured meringues takes up most of the window.

'It was nice to meet you,' says the woman. 'I'll know where to come in the future when I need my sugar fix.'

I don't answer for a moment. Can this really be Isabella – the annoying, stuck up, horsey snob? It seems highly unlikely. But it's definitely Stephen's car, so unless he's juggling a bewildering variety of tall, blonde paramours, this must be her.

The car horn beeps, and the possible Isabella looks annoyed. 'Just for that, he can wait.'

'He may be in a hurry,' I suggest.

'That's his problem! I don't answer car horns. My mum taught me early on that if someone wants to see you, they can jolly well come and get you.'

That's exactly the sort of thing families like hers teach you. My mother would jump out of her chair at the first indication someone wanted her. She hates keeping anyone waiting. Maybe that's why it never occurred to me to tell Stephen where to go when he used to beep his horn at me.

I feel a grudging admiration for this woman. On the other hand, I understand why Stephen arranged to meet her outside the shop rather than come in.

'We're about to close for lunch,' I say on a note of inspiration. 'My boss is very particular about closing on time.'

'Your sign says twelve thirty,' she says, and I groan inwardly. That's the worst of these expensive private schools – they teach you both literacy and numeracy. Why couldn't she have gone to the local comprehensive?

The horn sounds again, and she folds her arms. 'That does it. If he wants me to have lunch with him, he can come in and get me. If need be, I'll buy some more doughnuts to keep your boss happy.'

I manage a weak smile. She turns her back to the shop window and pretends to study our appetising selection of mini apple crumbles. I'm curious to see which of them wins this battle of wills. I secretly want it to be Isabella. When I was with Stephen, I didn't win a single one. To tell the truth, I barely tried. But if Stephen wins, it means he won't come into the shop, and I won't have to see him and his new girlfriend together.

Mr Mason comes bustling out of the office. 'Have you started closing up for lunch, Lily? You know we open again at one o'clock sharp.'

He sees Isabella. 'I beg your pardon. I didn't realise we had a customer. Please, take your time.'

Isabella gives him a charming smile. 'I'm trying to decide between an apple and a blackcurrant crumble. They both look delicious. Your assistant has been incredibly helpful.'

Before he can speak, a car door slams, and Stephen emerges onto the pavement. He opens the bakery door but doesn't come inside.

Isabella doesn't turn around, although she must be aware he's there.

Mr Mason recognises Stephen. 'Good morning, Mr Parker! How nice to see you back so soon. Is there anything we can help you with? Any special orders, or are you here to amend your previous order?'

He looks startled as I make a wild throat slashing gesture. I point to Isabella and lay a finger on my lips.

'Are you ready, Isabella?' says Stephen curtly.

She turns her head. 'Oh, are you here already? I wasn't expecting you so soon.'

He looks annoyed. 'We agreed to meet outside the shops at twelve thirty.'

'So we did,' she says coolly. 'But I was hungry, so I popped into the bakery. Are you a regular here?'

'Not at all,' he says with a glance at me that clearly says this state of affairs will continue as long as I'm working here.

'So, why do you have a special order?' she asks.

Stephen opens his mouth, then shuts it without speaking. Mr Mason still looks puzzled.

'It's for your mother, isn't it?' I improvise wildly. 'Doesn't she get her bread from us each week?'

Stephen gives me a grateful look. 'I believe she does. We really need to go. We have a table booked.'

Isabella smiles at me. 'Thanks for all your help. I expect I'll see you the next time my blood sugar gets low. I didn't catch your name.'

'Lily.' I watch her for any sign she recognises it.

She looks at me more closely, then back at Stephen, who looks profoundly embarrassed.

A slow smile creeps over her face. 'I know that name. Are you the Lily that Stephen used to date?'

She doesn't look remotely put out. I'd have found it difficult to bump into one of Stephen's exes when we were together. But she obviously doesn't see me as any kind of threat, even wearing my baggy flowered smock, with my hair attractively pulled back under a hairnet.

She holds out her hand. 'Nice to meet you, Lily. I'm Isabella.'

She laughs. 'We should have known we were talking about the same man.'

Mr Mason jangles his keys and coughs. 'If there's nothing else, we are about to close.'

'Of course,' says Stephen with a look of relief.

I pull off my hair net, pick up my coat and follow them outside. Mr Mason carefully locks up and sets off down the street at a brisk trot.

'He's in a hurry,' says Isabella.

'You shouldn't have kept him waiting,' says Stephen.

She shrugs. 'He can reopen a few minutes later if he wants. Do you really only get half an hour for lunch, Lily?'

'I do, so I should go. It's a ten-minute walk home.'

'You poor thing!' she says. 'That's absolutely ridiculous. Why don't you come to the pub with us?'

'No!' Stephen and I say simultaneously.

'It's very kind of you,' I add, 'but I won't gate crash your lunch. Besides, my mum's expecting me. But I hope you enjoy your steak and kidney pudding.'

She looks disappointed. 'That's a pity. Another time, perhaps.'

Judging by Stephen's expression, he won't be arranging to pick her up again within ten miles of here.

'Perhaps,' I say and set off as quickly as I can down the high street. As I turn to cross the road, I see them driving off in the direction of the pub.

I walk home in a daze. That was unexpected. If I hadn't found out who she was, I'd have thought she was really nice. I liked her amused eyes and quick sense of humour. Even more, I admired her refusal to dance to anyone else's tune.

In any other situation, she's someone I'd have liked to be friends with. As it is, I'll probably never see her again. Stephen will make sure of that. Just in case, I resolve to meet up with Jack as quickly as possible so we can get our stories straight.

Chapter Thirteen

I meet Jack for a drink after work on Wednesday. I would have preferred to see him sooner, but he said it was the earliest he could manage. I arrive a few minutes before him and buy the first round.

He rushes in a few minutes later. 'Hey, Lily, sorry we couldn't meet any earlier. I had a work thing on Monday night, and I had to meet a friend yesterday. Did you have a good day?'

I feel a flash of disappointment. Surely his girlfriend ought to be more of a priority than meeting some random friend, and certainly when she's in the middle of a crisis.

I check myself, remembering I'm not his actual girlfriend. Also, he's doing me a huge favour when he probably has a hundred other things he'd prefer to be doing. He lives in this area and has a life here, whereas I made the decision to leave.

I'm ashamed of my selfishness. I do this with my parents too, assuming they wait in some sort of limbo for my visits. I don't seriously expect that. I'm not that selfish, but I'm always taken by surprise when things change while I'm away. I resolve to find out more about what Jack's been up to over the past six months — once we've talked about our romance and got our stories straight.

'Lily?' he says, and I realise I was supposed to answer.

'I'm still here,' I say.

He looks amused. 'I know. I can hear you breathing. That sounded suspiciously like a deep sigh. What's up?'

'Nothing, apart from this stupid mess I've got myself into. And you, too.'

He laughs. 'You haven't got me into any kind of mess. I'm having fun.'

'I'm glad one of us is,' I say gloomily, then quickly add. 'I'm extremely grateful to you for agreeing to go along with it. I should never have done such a stupid thing in the first place.'

'Don't beat yourself up about it,' he says. 'What's done is done, and no one's being harmed by it.'

'Except you.'

'I told you. I'm having fun. Work's a bit dull at the moment, and this gives me something to do. Plenty of people dress up in medieval costumes and rush around enacting battles and learning how to use spinning wheels and whatever. This isn't too different.'

I blink. Is he comparing me to some old woman in medieval times? I decide not to pursue this.

'There's Mum and Dad too,' I say. 'They'll be devastated when we break up, even if they don't find out I lied to them.'

'They'll be fine,' he reassures me. 'I'm fine as a fake boyfriend, but they'd absolutely hate having me as a son-in-law.'

'That's not true! They love you.'

'They love everyone,' he says. 'But they wouldn't want you to stay with someone who isn't a good fit for you.'

I'm not sure what he means. They weren't at all surprised when they heard Jack and I had got together, which must mean they think we're a good fit.

'Lily?' he says. 'Are you still with me?'

'I was thinking about what you said about my parents. They'll be upset when I tell them. I need to think of a plausible reason to break up with you.'

'I could give you several,' he says. 'If you prefer, I could make up some truly terrible secrets about myself that will leave you with no choice but to dump me at once and run back to London.'

'They wouldn't believe me,' I say. 'They already know what a nice guy you are. And you don't deserve that. I'll think of something and hope for the best. You have to live here when I've left. I don't want to trash your reputation.'

'Some women like bad boys,' he says. 'I may be inundated with beautiful women trying to tame me. In the meantime, I'll put up with you. Speaking of being a good boyfriend, your birthday is coming up. What would you like to do for it?'

I groan. 'Nothing at all. I want to forget all about it. I feel guilty enough about all this without allowing people to make a fuss of me.'

'So, you should,' he says severely. 'You should be ashamed of yourself. But can I point out that your parents will expect your amazing new boyfriend to arrange something incredible for the love of his life on her special day?'

'You could say you're working,' I suggest.

'They'd only expect us to do something another day. I'm afraid you're stuck with me for your birthday celebration. You'll have to make the best of it.'

There's no one with whom I'd rather spend my birthday, but I feel increasingly guilty about all this. It was lovely of Jack to agree so readily to this complete farce. Maybe he's telling the truth and is having fun. But there has to be a limit to what I ask of him.

'We'll find something or other to do that night,' I say. 'But I'm paying.'

'McDonald's, it is!' he says. 'I'll start getting myself into training.'

'I think I can run to somewhere a little more special than that. I have my redundancy money, and my parents absolutely refuse to take rent from me. Where would you like to go?'

He considers. 'If we're talking hypothetically, there's an amazing new place called The Oasis all the critics are raving about. It would be cool to say we'd tried it.'

'Let's do it!' I say. 'Don't worry about the cost. I'd love to take you there to say thank you for being so great about all this.'

He bursts out laughing. 'Are you kidding? It isn't the price, although I imagine you'd need a mortgage just to buy one of their starters. That place is booked out for about a year ahead. You could probably get in if you were a cabinet minister or a film star. But the likes of us have to go on a waiting list and still risk being turned down when we arrive, in case we jeopardise one of their precious Michelin stars.'

'That's a shame,' I say, deflated. 'I'd have loved to take you there. We can put our names down anyway, and I can come home when we finally get in.'

'Maybe,' he says, with less enthusiasm than I would have expected. 'Anyway, we'll have to choose somewhere else this year. Does your family have anything planned?'

'Not that I'm aware of. Mum loves birthdays, so I expect she'll want to go out for lunch. It's lucky it falls on a Sunday, so I don't have to work.'

Jack picks up our glasses. 'This is my round. Same again?'

'Thanks.'

He heads towards the bar, and I think about Sunday. It will be lovely to spend the evening with Jack. I hope he didn't have anything else planned. Perhaps we can't go to The Oasis, but there must be somewhere almost as nice. He deserves it, and as he pointed out, Mum and Dad will expect it. Whatever he thinks, they'll be sad to lose him. Who wouldn't want their daughter to meet someone like Jack? He's kind and generous and hard working – every parent's dream.

I'll wait to tell them until Stephen's gone back to Manchester, but I don't want the news of our breakup getting around the village too quickly. If Stephen's mother hears it and relays it to him, he may put two and two together and make some ridiculous and completely unwarranted number.

I'll have to leave it for a respectable period before announcing it. I may find myself a new job soon. If so, I can tell my parents I don't want to turn down the job, and Jack doesn't want to move. It's simply a matter of competing priorities.

Jack returns with the drinks. 'You look very serious. What are you thinking about?'

'Our breakup,' I say.

He hands me a glass. 'I can understand that. It must be hard to let go of such a catch. Personally, I don't think I could do it.'

'Especially such a modest one,' I agree. 'We'll cross that bridge when we come to it. At least, I will.'

'And I'll be at home licking my wounds,' he says. 'But I'll enjoy it while it lasts.'

I pull out a notebook and pencil. 'Shall we get to work while I'm sober enough to spell correctly?'

'Great idea,' he says. 'We must get our entire backstory correct. Every single detail. We can't risk even the tiniest mistake.'

'I don't think we need to worry too much,' I say. 'A rough outline will do.'

'Not at all,' he insists. 'Even the smallest discrepancy could ruin everything. I need to know the colour of your second favourite duvet cover and your favourite brand of toothpaste – assuming I'm in a position to know that. Do I spend the night at yours when I visit London? Do you use sheets and blankets instead of a duvet? It's an absolute minefield. You'll need several more notebooks.'

I can't believe how seriously he's taking this. This is a side of him I've never seen before.

'Jack,' I begin, then catch sight of his face. 'You're winding me up. I should have known.'

'You should indeed. I think we can get away with a broad outline. We know each other pretty well, which makes it easier.

All the rest – those delightful, romantic details which make falling in love so special – can come later.'

I take a gulp of my drink. 'I'll need several more of these before you get any delightful, personal details from me.'

'I'm disappointed,' he says. 'I'd hoped we were taking our relationship to a whole new level. You may come around when you see how open and vulnerable I'm prepared to make myself. My favourite brand of toothpaste is Colgate, extra minty. And when I was eight, I told my parents it was my sister who had eaten the last slice of chocolate cake, when in fact it was me. I even watched them send her to her room for an hour without lifting a finger to save her. I only hope you can continue to love me after such shocking revelations.'

I open the notebook. 'I'll try to remember you were very young and forget the rest. It won't be easy, but if this relationship is worth fighting for, I'm prepared to do my part.'

'Me too,' he says cheerfully. 'I already know about the time you told your parents you had a special advanced history class on a Saturday so you could meet that boy they didn't approve of, and I'm still willing to be your boyfriend. So, we're off to an excellent start.'

He picks up his glass and inspects the dregs. 'I'll need another of these in a minute. But first, let's drink a toast.'

I pick up my glass. 'What shall we drink to?'

'To everlasting love,' he suggests.

'Let's not get carried away.'

'What, then?'

'To friendship,' I say. 'It may not be as romantic as true love, but it lasts a lot longer.'

'Fine,' he says. 'I'll drink to friendship! And to my best friend putting away that ridiculous notebook, taking out her purse, and organising the next round.'

Chapter Fourteen

I wake the following morning with a throbbing headache. At least, Mum wakes me.

'Up you get, sleepyhead!' she trills as she opens my door.

I groan, roll over, and pull the pillow over my head. 'Go away. It's far too early.'

She snaps on the bedroom light. 'It's seven o'clock. You need some breakfast before you go to work.'

I resist the urge to hurl the pillow at her. It's kind of her to get up specially to make me breakfast. I've tried several times to persuade her there's no need, but she's determined.

She looks at me with concern. 'Oh, dear. You do look rough. Do you think you're going down with something? Shall I call Mr Mason?'

I swing my legs off the bed. 'No, don't do that. I'm a bit … dehydrated.'

There's a loud guffaw. Ben is walking down the landing and has overheard us. 'Dehydrated? More like hungover.'

I debate throwing the pillow at him, but it might hit Mum. I content myself with glaring at him instead. 'I'm starting to understand why Mia left you.'

He turns on his heel and stalks off. Mum gives me a shocked look. 'What a terrible thing to say, Lily.'

She's right. That was completely uncalled for.

'I'll go and apologise,' I say, pushing my feet into my slippers.

She lowers her voice. 'I'd wait until he's eaten. You know what your brother's like in the morning.'

I do indeed. Ben has been a byword for the perils of low blood sugar for as long as I can remember. He's a pleasant, easy-going guy, but if you catch him before a meal, you take your life into your own hands. Which is still no excuse for what I said to him.

I pick up my towel. 'I'll take a shower and see you downstairs.'

Ben is already at the breakfast table when I come in. He doesn't look up. I touch his shoulder as I pass. 'I'm sorry, Ben. I didn't mean it.'

He nods in acknowledgement but doesn't speak. Mum bustles in with a dish of bacon and eggs.

'There you go, sweetheart,' she says to Ben. 'You'll feel much better once you've got that inside you.'

'I was planning on having toast,' he says. 'I'm in a hurry. I can take it with me if I don't finish it.'

'Good idea,' says Mum. 'I'll bring it through.'

She disappears, and I remember my jam eating marathon yesterday. I was hoping Ben would ask for toast today and be upset to discover his favourite plum jam had all gone. But that was before I behaved like an idiot and spoke to him so unkindly.

'Why not have the bacon and eggs now they're ready?' I say. 'It's much better for you in the morning than toast.'

'No, it isn't,' he counters.

That's Ben all over. If you want him to do something, suggest he does the opposite, and you end up with your preferred outcome. I should have extolled the virtues of simple carbohydrates. That would have had him reaching for the eggs in no time.

'Yes, it is,' I say. 'I was reading an article about eating protein in the morning. Apparently, it helps you to stay full longer.'

'Go ahead,' he says.

'I don't have time. I'm already running late. Why don't you eat this, and I'll take the toast to go?'

'Because I'm having the toast,' he says. 'Mum can make some more for you. Better still, why don't you make it yourself?'

I bite back a sharp retort. I don't want to upset him any further. 'Maybe I will. You could try honey on your toast for once. I read this article where –'

'People who eat honey live an average of ten years longer?' he interrupts. 'I'm sure you did, but I'll take my chances.'

Mum comes through with the toast, and Ben grabs a handful of slices. 'Thanks, Mum. Do we have any plum jam?'

She looks worried. 'I opened the cupboard to get it for you, but I couldn't find it. Your father must have put it somewhere ridiculous, as usual.'

I cram a piece of bacon into my mouth and finish my coffee. 'I have to go. Mr Mason wants to show me the ordering procedure this morning.'

Mum claps her hands. 'Oh, Lily, how marvellous! He must think a lot of you if he's showing you the ropes so soon.'

I leave the room, but not quickly enough to avoid hearing Ben's derisive snort.

I arrive at work a minute before Mr Mason and wait outside the shop, feeling smug. For all he knows, I've been waiting here for hours, eager to crack the mysteries of the bakery business.

He comes trudging up the street exactly on time. He looks tired, which is unusual. I don't know him well enough to ask whether anything is wrong. Mum would, but she gets away with talking about the most personal of issues to people she barely knows. They seem to sense her boundless store of goodwill towards humanity and respond to her. I haven't inherited that trait from her, and neither has Ben. We're more like Dad – slightly reserved until we get to know someone.

Mr Mason and I go about our morning tasks in silence. Once we've set up the shop, and he's confident no burglars have been in during the night to throw a custard slice and lemon muffin rave, he disappears into his office, leaving me in charge.

I have mixed feelings about this. I'm terrified of doing something wrong. But I enjoy the feeling of power it gives me and spend a while amusing myself by pretending I own the business and have the right to reject unpleasant customers with dogs. Not Bernard, though. He has a cheeky glint in his eye I rather like.

But I could refuse to allow his owner inside. I could insist she waited in the street and sent Bernard in with a note. I could also ban any tall, dark-haired men making unreasonable requests that we alter our perfectly good products to fit in with some ridiculous Hallmark holiday.

The door opens, and I look up expectantly. I'm surprised to see Isabella.

She smiles when she sees me. 'I'm glad it's you. I came in on Sunday morning, and your boss served me. He was most put out that I didn't know the difference between a ciabatta and a baguette. My mum asked me to pick one of those long loaf things, and I thought he'd be bound to know what I meant.'

'I had no idea we sold baguettes,' I confess.

'I don't think you do. He seemed to think I was making fun of his bakery. I almost asked for a sourdough focaccia, but I thought better of it.'

I can't help warming to her. She may be dating my ex-boyfriend, but that isn't technically a crime or even a moral failing.

'Are you here to buy another long loaf?' I ask. 'Or are you after our doughnuts?'

Her eyes light up. 'Now, there's an idea. I had breakfast almost an hour ago, so it could count as elevenses.'

She looks around the shop. 'It must be fun working here, eating as many cakes as you want.'

'The staff isn't allowed to eat the products,' I say. 'It may seem small and unimportant at first, but it quickly leads to further abuses, and very soon the bottom line is affected.'

She gives a snort of laughter. 'Does he really say that?'

'That, and many other things. You wouldn't believe what a complicated business it is running an outfit like this, nor how many rules we have.'

'It's good to expand my education,' she says. 'But I think I'll stick to accounts. I didn't come in for anything special today. I wanted to ask whether you'd like to have lunch sometime.'

She laughs at my startled look. 'Not to discuss Stephen — although it would be fun to compare notes. I thought it would be nice to get to know you. Loads of my friends have moved away from the village, and I don't know many people around here.'

I stare at her, my mind racing. There must be more to this request than appears on the surface. Why would anyone choose to get to know their boyfriend's ex-girlfriend? It's clear she doesn't see me as a threat, and it's equally clear why. But it's less obvious why she would want to spend any more time with me than she has to.

She watches me, an enquiring look on her face. 'Only if you'd like to. You don't need to decide now. Give me your phone.'

I don't move. Why is this complete stranger demanding my phone? Is this show of friendliness a pretext to get my phone away from me and check whether Stephen and I are still in contact?

She seems to read my thoughts. 'Here's my phone. Put your number into it, and I'll send you a text. That way, we'll have each other's details.'

'Oh, yes. Good idea.' I take her phone and type my number into it, then hand it back.

'Great!' she says, tapping the keys.

My phone pings, and I reach for it, wondering who could be texting me during work hours.

I am not a mad stalker!

I look up at her and see she's laughing. 'Message me sometime if you'd like to get lunch. It's awful that you only get half an hour, but we could go to the pub. If you let me know what you'd like to eat, I could order it before you arrive.'

I nod, bewildered by the speed at which events have overtaken me. I wonder whether Stephen knows she's here. Is this his idea? I'm sure it isn't. He seemed uncomfortable being in the same place with us on Monday. The last thing he'd want would be to engineer another meeting between us, especially one involving alcohol.

'See you around,' she says and turns to leave.

On a sudden impulse, I say. 'I'm free today if that works for you.'

'Fantastic!' she says with what sounds like genuine enthusiasm. 'I'll meet you at the Red Lion at twelve thirty. The menu's online, so choose what you want and message me ahead of time. This one's on me, so feel free to go for the lobster.'

She waves and disappears. I watch her walk along the high street, not sure what to make of it all. No one asks to meet their boyfriend's ex-girlfriend without an ulterior motive. I have no idea what it is, but I suppose I'm about to find out.

Chapter Fifteen

I arrive out of breath a few minutes after twelve thirty and find Isabella waiting for me.

She greets me with a huge smile. 'You made it!'

'Did you think I wouldn't?' I ask, accepting the glass of mulled wine she hands me and deciding Mr Mason will have to take his chances on my accuracy with the till this afternoon.

'I thought the old curmudgeon might demand you work right through lunch,' she says.

'He isn't a curmudgeon,' I say. 'He's just fussy.'

She takes a gulp of her wine. 'Anyone who allows his staff half an hour for lunch counts as a curmudgeon in my book.'

'He only takes half an hour himself,' I point out.

'That's his business,' she says. 'I can't think why you work there.'

Our food arrives, which saves me having to answer. How much does she know about me? Has Stephen told her everything or nothing? He may consider me to be so far in his past that I don't count at all.

'I told you when we first met that I lost my job in London,' I say.

'I know you did. But that doesn't explain why you're working in a bakery.' She crams several chips into her mouth and chews rapidly.

I feel a wave of annoyance. Of course, someone like this can't understand why regular people need to work for a living. She probably doesn't work full time in her family business but goes in for a few hours whenever she feels like it. It's probably a tax break for them. Even the concept of having a family business shows she hasn't the faintest idea of how ordinary people live.

'It's a temporary thing,' I say at last. 'I'm looking for a new job in London.'

'What do you do?' she asks.

So, she and Stephen haven't discussed me. I'm not sure whether to be pleased or annoyed.

'I'm an office manager,' I say.

'Do you enjoy it?'

I pause with a forkful of fried cod halfway to my mouth, not sure how to answer. Most people say things like, 'That must be interesting,' or, 'That sounds like fun.' They take it for granted that I enjoy it.

'It pays well,' I say, 'and there's a good career structure.'

'But do you enjoy it?' she persists.

Why is she asking all these questions? She can't be interested in the life of a woman she's only just met. Is Stephen behind this, after all? Has he asked her to dig out all the information she can about me and my new life? Does that mean he's still interested in me and what I get up to?

My wave of euphoria dies as quickly as it arrived. This has nothing to do with Stephen. He isn't sneaky like that. If he wanted to know something, he would ask me directly. For another thing, he's seeing Isabella now. He wouldn't use her like that, and she wouldn't allow it. Reluctant though I am to admit it, she seems smart. She would see straight through him if he tried it. So, she must be asking for another reason, although I can't for the life of me imagine what it is.

I decide to hedge until I've worked out her motivation. 'I enjoy my job. It's interesting and varied.'

'More so than working at the bakery?' There's a definite note of amusement in her voice that raises my hackles.

'Beggars can't be choosers,' I say. 'We don't all have family money to fall back on.'

She regards me with what looks like fascination. 'Is that what you think? That I come from family money?'

I didn't expect such a direct attack. I hoped she might have taken the hint and backed off.

'I assumed you did,' I say. 'Stephen told me his new girlfriend lived in the Manor House in Little Compton. It's a pretty swish place.'

'It is,' she says, 'but we live at the Lodge. It's the house near the gates. You can see it from the road.'

'Who lives in the main house?' I ask.

'Our cousins. Dad's older brother owns the farm. That's how it goes in farming families.'

My hackles rise at the thought of Ben inheriting our family business, simply because he's the oldest. Not that we have a family business, but the point still stands.

'That seems incredibly unfair,' I say.

'I can see how you'd think so,' she agrees, 'but it's the way it's usually done in farming. Otherwise, all the farms would be broken up, which wouldn't work at all. I don't think Dad minds too much. We get to live in the Lodge, and we don't have any of the worries associated with running the farm. Dad only works part time now, whereas I doubt my uncle will ever retire. None of his children want to go into farming, so I suppose the farm will have to be sold when he dies.'

I finish the rest of my fish and chips in silence. I may have rushed to judgement a little too quickly. But even if her family aren't massive landowners, that doesn't mean I have to like her.

'Where did you go to school?' I ask.

'The Grange.'

Ha! I knew she must have gone to the Grange!

Something of what I'm thinking must show on my face because she smiles.

'We were pretty lucky. My parents could never have afforded it, but my uncle chipped in, and I had a partial scholarship.'

'My brother and I went to Bournefield Comp,' I say, watching her for any sign of derision.

She sighs. 'I wanted to go there. All my friends from primary school did. But my parents thought it was too good an opportunity to miss.'

'What was it like at The Grange?'

'It was fine. There's something to enjoy in most places if you put your mind to it.'

'Like the bakery?' I say, and she laughs.

'I expect so. What are your three favourite things about working there?'

I frown in concentration. How am I meant to come up with even one nice thing to say about the Sugarloaf? But Isabella looks expectant, and I don't want to disappoint her.

'It's an easy walking distance from my parents' house,' I say with a burst of inspiration.

She gives me an encouraging smile. 'That's a good one. I expect you had a long commute in London?'

'I did. Over an hour. It's alright in the summer, but not so much fun in the winter.'

'What else?' she says.

'You sound like my mother,' I grumble. 'Fine, I quite like chatting with the customers. In my last job, I was stuck in a tiny cubicle well away from the main offices, and I never got to see anyone except during meetings.'

'There you go!' she says.

I give her a reluctant smile. 'I'll admit it isn't as bad as it could have been if that makes you happy.'

'I tell you what would make me happy – some of Ted's treacle tart and custard. Just the thing for a chilly day.'

'I have to be back at work in twelve minutes,' I protest.

'No problem,' she says. 'I pre-ordered it. Here it is!'

Sure enough, I see a server approaching us carrying two steaming bowls. I look at the golden, syrupy tart and thick yellow custard and give in.

'You're going to lose me my job,' I say, picking up my spoon.

She waits until I've taken my first mouthful before asking. 'What are you doing this weekend?'

'I'm working on Saturday. It's my birthday on Sunday, so I'll be going out for dinner.'

'With your boyfriend?' she asks.

I can't remember whether I've talked to her about Jack. Stephen may have mentioned him to reassure her that she shouldn't be concerned about my presence in the village. Not that she seems in the slightest bit threatened. Looking at the pair of us, I can kind of see why.

'Uh huh,' I mumble, pretending to be deeply interested in getting the perfect ratio of custard to treacle tart onto my spoon.

'That's nice,' she says. 'How long have you been seeing him?'

I try to remember what I told Stephen about my wonderful new relationship. I ought to write myself a timeline and memorise it. I didn't expect anyone to find out about it, let alone interrogate me at every opportunity about the intricate details.

'Nearly a year,' I say.

'So, you met soon after you and Stephen broke up?'

What is it with this woman and her questions? She has Stephen, and I don't. Isn't that enough for her?

I decide to carry the battle into her territory. 'How long have you and Stephen been seeing each other?'

'About three or four months,' she says.

What does she mean by 'about?' How does she not know how long she's been seeing him? I knew to the day how long he and I were together. If I can give the date of my fictional relationship to within a week, she ought to remember the exact date she started seeing Stephen.

'Not long,' I say, relieved to find he didn't go straight from me to her.

'Not at all,' she agrees. 'It's early days with us. We're still getting to know each other. We only met at the end of September, and he moved to Manchester after Christmas.'

'But he came all the way down here to visit you for Valentine's Day. That must mean he's serious.'

She laughs. 'He came home to see his parents for a couple of weeks. His father hasn't been well. The trip happened to coincide with Valentine's Day. I don't think he's romantic enough to have made a special trip.'

I debate whether to tell her he took me away to the Lake District last Valentine's Day. I don't need to mention that he broke up with me straight afterwards. It isn't relevant.

'He's not the most romantic person I've ever met,' I say. 'But he has a kind heart, which is more important.'

'Possibly,' she says. 'But wouldn't you rather have both?'

'In a perfect world. But you can't have everything. If you hold out for perfection, you may end up with nothing.'

'True, but he'd better have something nice planned for Valentine's Day,' she says cheerfully. 'Men can be so lazy.'

I think of the cookies he's ordered and wonder whether that counts as romantic in her book. Especially when iced by her predecessor. I almost warn her not to get her hopes up but stop myself. The cookies may be part of a larger overall plan – an *amuse-bouche* before the actual celebration begins, like the twelve days of Christmas.

For all I know, he's planning to whisk her away for a day of amazing romantic treats. He may have booked a couple's treatment at a spa, followed by hot air ballooning over the New Forest, accompanied at a discreet distance by a fighter jet escort. After which, he'll whisk her away in a limousine to a country hotel for a five-course meal with champagne to be eaten in their luxury suite next to a rose-petal covered four poster bed.

I wrench my thoughts away from the movie playing in my head. I'm not going there.

'What's he like, this new boyfriend of yours?' she asks.

I'm tempted to tell her to mind her own business, but I don't have the heart. She looks eager and interested, like a puppy. This could be an excellent opportunity to practise getting my story straight before I have to tell it to anyone who matters, by which I mean Stephen.

'Erm, five foot ten, brown hair –' I begin.

She laughs. 'I don't mean what does he look like? What's he like as a person?'

This one is trickier to answer. When you talk about someone you barely know, you have to use your brain. When you talk about someone you know almost as well as yourself, you simply feel them without needing to put their essence into words. Still, I should try.

'He's lovely,' I begin, then stop. She's looking for something more specific than that. A rose is lovely. A sunset is lovely.

I try again. 'He's the kindest man I've ever met.'

Should I say except for Stephen? I don't want to sound as though I'm denigrating him to his new girlfriend. I decide not to refer to Stephen. It's a potential mine field, and I don't trust myself to talk about him with believable indifference. It would be the height of humiliation if my voice were to wobble when I mentioned his name.

'He makes me laugh more than anyone I know,' I say, smiling at the memory of Jack's face when he's teasing me.

She sighs. 'That's so important. I could forgive almost anything in a man who makes me laugh.'

Does Stephen make her laugh? If so, he must show her a different side of himself to the one he showed me. I loved Stephen deeply. I still do. But his sense of humour was never his overriding quality. He had plenty of good points to make up for it. He was charming and intelligent and driven, and when I was with him, he made me feel as though I was the only other person in the world. He gave me his entire focus, and I felt I was the only thing that mattered to him.

Does he make Isabella feel that way? He must do. She isn't the sort of person who would settle for anything less. I remember with admiration how she forced him to come into the bakery to collect her.

But we aren't talking about Stephen. We're talking about Jack. It's impossible to describe him to someone who's never met him. How can I put into words his zest for life, his infectious laugh, the way he looks at the world in a slightly different way to me but still closely enough for us to connect, so that I end up seeing things from a new and exciting perspective?

How can I explain the way he takes me seriously but makes me believe there's never anything that can't be fixed? I think of the way his grey-green eyes light up when he's interested or amused, his ready smile, his ability to make everyone around him feel comfortable in their own skin.

I look up and meet Isabella's interested gaze. 'He's great,' I say.

'He sounds it,' she says, and we both laugh.

'It's more difficult than you'd think to describe someone you know so well,' I say.

'I wasn't trying to be nosy,' she says. 'I'm just interested in people. By the way, where is this paragon taking you for your birthday dinner?'

Jack's last suggestion was McDonald's, but it might be better not to mention that.

'I expect we'll find somewhere,' I say. 'Jack was telling me he wants to go to The Oasis, but they're booked up for months ahead, as well as being hideously expensive.'

Her face lights up. 'Does he really want to eat there? I might be able to help you. My uncle's friend is the head chef, and he often does my uncle a favour. Would you like me to see whether I can get you a table for Sunday night?'

I gape at her, stunned. Jack would love that. It would be great to take him somewhere special to thank him for taking part in this ridiculous charade.

'If that's a serious offer, I'd love to take you up on it,' I say. 'But it's such short notice.'

'I can't promise anything,' she warns me. 'I'll do what I can and let you know.'

'I have to go now, or I'll be fired,' I say. 'I can't tell you how grateful I am. It's fine if you can't get us a table. I'm sure we'll find somewhere else.'

'I'll call now,' she says, pulling out her phone. 'Don't worry. I usually manage to get what I want. Perseverance is the key.'

She may be right. She certainly managed to get my boyfriend. I pull myself up short. She did nothing of the kind. She happened to meet someone who was single, and she started a relationship with him. I'm finding it increasingly difficult to feel resentment towards her.

It wasn't Stephen's fault, either. I may not like the way things have turned out, but it's time I stopped behaving like a petulant child over the whole thing.

I give her a quick wave and head for the door, thinking of Jack. I shouldn't get my hopes up too much, but I can't help feeling excited. I won't tell him where we're going. Jack is rarely lost for words, and I'd like to enjoy surprising him.

Chapter Sixteen

Mum asks me that evening what I'd like to do for my birthday.

'Dad and I thought we might take you to Massimo's for dinner,' she says. 'But that was before we knew about you and Jack. I'm sure the pair of you are looking forward to a nice romantic evening together.'

I give her an uncomfortable smile. 'We're planning to have dinner on Sunday.'

'Of course, you are,' she says with a beaming smile. 'You never forget the first birthday you spend with the love of your life.'

I lift a hand in protest. 'Let's not get carried away. Jack isn't the love of my life, and I'm definitely not his. We're casually dating, that's all. It probably won't work out between us.'

She tips her head on one side. 'I don't think so. You're absolutely perfect for each other. Dad and I were saying that only last night. Neither of us could understand why we hadn't thought of it before.'

'Don't say that to Jack,' I warn her. 'You'll terrify him!'

'I wouldn't be so daft. I'm saying it to you.'

'And I'm telling you that you're way ahead of yourself,' I say. 'Honestly, Mum. It's nothing. I don't want you and Dad getting upset if it doesn't work out.'

She hands me some cutlery. 'Set the table, please. And don't be so ridiculous. This has nothing to do with me and Dad. All we want is for you to be happy. If Jack isn't the right person for you, that's fine.'

At least I've warned her I don't see this as anything serious. It would look odd if I pushed the subject any further. People in the first flush of a new relationship aren't usually expecting it to end.

'We can do something as a family during the day,' I say. 'Maybe we could go out to lunch.'

'If you're sure,' she says. 'Why don't you find out what Jack wants to do first?'

I remember Isabella and her approach to relationships.

'It isn't important what Jack wants to do,' I say. 'It's my birthday, and I want to have lunch with my family. I'm sure Jack will cope without me until the evening.'

'Unless he'd like to come with us?' she says.

Usually, I'd be happy for Jack to join us for a family lunch, but not this year. I can't bear a repeat of last Sunday evening, with my parents watching me and Jack as though we were interesting specimens at a zoo and they a couple of anthropologists making notes on our mating behaviours.

'It will be nice to spend some time with you and Dad,' I say. 'Ben too, if he wants to come along.'

'As long as you don't say anything unkind about him and Mia,' she warns me.

'I won't,' I promise. 'Is she likely to be around? We could invite her too.'

'Now, there's an idea,' she says. 'I wonder why I didn't think of it before. I'll suggest it to Ben.'

I lay the table, then return to the kitchen to see what I can do to help. Mum doesn't allow me to do anything important, but she lets me stir the sauce.

'The trick is to stir it slowly, but constantly,' she says. 'If you do it too fast, it will splash. If you do it too slowly, you risk it catching on the bottom of the pan.'

'I'll do my best,' I promise.

I stir the sauce for a few minutes before asking. 'Did you and Dad say the same thing about me and Stephen when we were together? That we were perfect for each other, I mean.'

Is it my imagination, or does Mum's face turn pink? Maybe it's the heat of the stove.

'I'm not sure we had that exact conversation,' she says, not looking at me directly.

'Why not?' I ask. 'Didn't you like him?'

She looks shocked. 'Naturally, we liked him! He's a lovely young man.'

'It sounds as though there's a 'but' in there somewhere.'

She switches off the potatoes, which are threatening to boil over. 'It's just that it wasn't as immediately obvious to us why you two were together. But Stephen made you happy, which was all we cared about. So, it comes to the same thing.'

'He did make me happy,' I say. 'He still would.'

Her eyes are sympathetic as she considers me. 'But that's all over now. You broke up a long time ago, and you told us he's seeing someone else.'

She brightens. 'You've found someone new too, and he seems to make you very happy. You aren't still thinking of Stephen?'

'Of course not!' I say rather too vehemently, and she gives me a worried look.

'Not at all,' I say more calmly. 'I was only wondering why you weren't as enthusiastic about Stephen as you are about Jack. It doesn't matter.'

'Things work out the way they're meant to,' she says. 'I've always said that. And that's what happened with you and Jack. Now, if only Ben and Mia would start talking again, I'm sure they could work everything out. However, it's none of my business, and I don't intend to interfere.'

'Except for inviting Mia to my birthday lunch,' I tease her.

'That's different,' she says.

I let it drop. At least she isn't focusing on the many perfections of Jack and the rather fewer perfections of Stephen. I always felt she was slightly uncomfortable around Stephen, although I never knew why. If he and I had stayed together, she would have had more opportunity to get to know him. I'm confident she would have come to love him as much, if not more, than Jack.

The rest of the week passes quickly. I'm busy at work, although not with customers. Mr Mason insists on teaching me the intricacies of his bookkeeping method, which seems to have come straight out of some *Business for Beginners* course from the 1950s. He uses ruled ledgers and favours the double entry method of bookkeeping. I try to persuade him all this would be far easier on a computer, but he gives me a worried look.

'I've heard terrible tales about people losing all their information on computers. I couldn't risk it.'

'Nowadays, everything gets saved automatically to the cloud,' I assure him.

'What sort of cloud?' he says.

'It isn't an actual cloud. It's just an expression. Your information wouldn't only be on your computer. It would be saved on someone else's server.'

He looks even more confused. 'Who would be serving it?'

Too late, I realise this was the wrong word to use to explain the intricacies of data storage to someone whose only thought is of serving his customers.

'It doesn't matter,' I say. 'I'm quite happy to accept whatever method you prefer.'

'The old methods are best,' he says. 'Everyone chases after the newfangled ways of doing things, but they always come back to where it all started.'

By this reasoning, he ought to be inscribing his accounts on papyrus by the flickering light of a tallow candle. I'm about to comment but remember in time my resolve to be a little ray of sunshine around the workplace.

'I should sort out the out-of-date cream cakes,' I say.

'Good idea,' he says. 'We can't have our customers eating anything that might give them food poisoning.'

I'd be more than prepared to risk it, but I know better than to raise the subject again. The last time I mentioned taking the out-of-date cakes home, he reacted as though I'd suggested spreading cholera throughout the village.

I'm surprised and touched at closing time when he appears holding a cake.

'Your mother told me it's your birthday tomorrow,' he says. 'I wanted to give you something to show my appreciation of all your hard work. I didn't know what you'd like, but this seemed appropriate.'

I take the cake he hands me, trying not to laugh. He's obviously been inspired by Stephen's request because he's used the tip of a knife to scratch *Happy Birthday Lily* into the vanilla frosting. At least, I think that's what it says. Several of the letters have run into each other, and his writing is spidery at the best of times. For all I know, he meant to write *You're Fired*.

'Thank you very much, Mr Mason,' I say. 'I very much appreciate having this job.'

He looks pleased. 'Off you go. Enjoy your day tomorrow. Give my kindest regards to your mother.'

I set off down the street, clutching my cake. It's surprisingly heavy, and I wonder what it's filled with. We don't sell family size cakes. We order them in if our customers request it. He must have put in a special order for this one, which was kind of him.

'What have you got there?' says Mum as I walk in.

I lay the box on the table. 'Mr Mason gave me a cake.'

She looks at it in dismay. 'But I spent all afternoon making your favourite coffee and walnut cake.'

I switch on the kettle. 'I should hope so! Nothing beats your coffee and walnut cake. But there's nothing wrong with having two.'

'I suppose so,' she says. 'What flavour is this one?'

I peer at it again. 'I have no idea. It has vanilla icing, but it could be anything underneath. It's extremely heavy. Maybe it's not a cake at all. He may have iced a gold bar for me as a delightful surprise.'

'I wouldn't think so,' says Mum. 'He can't be making much money out of that shop.'

'Have you decided where you'd like to go tomorrow?' I ask, abandoning the subject of my cake and its possible contents.

'Let's go to Massimo's for lunch,' she says. 'We've never been there, and we hear good things.'

'That sounds lovely,' I say. 'I won't go hungry tomorrow.'

'Do you know where Jack's taking you yet?' she asks with interest.

'Actually, I'm taking Jack,' I say. 'But it's a secret. I'll tell you when I get home.'

She looks surprised. 'I hope he's paying.'

I'm about to tell her this one is on me, but I stop myself in time. It would involve an explanation I'm not prepared to give. Better to allow her to think this is a romantic meal and Jack is paying. She's hardly likely to demand the receipt when he drops me home.

My phone rings after dinner. I look at the screen and see Jack's name. 'I'll be back in a minute.'

Mum and Dad exchange glances that say only too clearly they think I need privacy to murmur sweet nothings down the phone line. Not the phone line, exactly. My words of love will bounce straight up to a satellite whizzing around somewhere above the atmosphere, then beam down to Jack as if by magic. Mr Mason would be horribly confused.

'Hi, Jack,' I say as soon as I'm out of earshot. 'I've booked us a table for tomorrow evening.'

'So have I,' he says. 'Isn't it the part of a loving boyfriend to make birthday arrangements?'

'Usually, it would be. But as you are neither loving nor a boyfriend, we can dispense with formalities. I'd rather go to my restaurant if you don't mind.'

'You don't know where I've booked,' he says. 'I know I promised you McDonald's, but I discovered in the interim that Burger King has a special two-for-one deal on onion rings this weekend only.'

'Tempting though that sounds, I'd prefer to stick with my original arrangements. Do you mind picking me up? I could borrow Mum's car, but ...'

'No, you couldn't,' he interrupts. 'Have you no romance in your soul? I'll be there on time, wearing my smartest outfit. I expect your father will want a word with me about manly things before we leave. Does he own a shot gun?'

I giggle. 'I think Ben has his old BB gun somewhere around. Will that do?'

'I suppose it will have to. Speaking of being on time, can you be precise?'

I think rapidly. 'Our table is booked for eight o'clock. It's half an hour's drive from here, and we'll want a drink first. How about seven o'clock? I'll see you then.'

'Is that it?' he asks. 'No loving words, no promises of eternal faithfulness? I'm not sure your heart is entirely in this relationship.'

'You're my very favourite Jack in the entire world,' I say. 'Will that do?'

He sighs. 'It's a start. I'm off to write a sonnet about your beauty. Dare I hope you'll be doing the same?'

'I'll write you a limerick about your ears. It's the best I can offer.'

He sighs again. 'Beggars can't be choosers. I bet you can't find a rhyme for seashell.'

'Challenge accepted,' I say. 'See you tomorrow. Don't be late!'

'Listen to the pair of us!' he says. 'We're like an old married couple.'

And he rings off before I can answer.

Chapter Seventeen

Jack arrives exactly on time on Sunday evening. I've already decided not to rush out to the car as I used to do with Stephen. I'm taking a leaf out of Isabella's book from now on. If Jack beeps his horn at me, he can stay out there and freeze to death.

But he comes to the front door, carrying a bunch of flowers. 'Happy Birthday, Lily!'

'Thanks,' I say. 'Are these for me? They're lovely.'

He holds them away from me. 'They're for your father.'

'Dad?' I say, puzzled.

'Of course. McCall's book of dating etiquette says you should always obtain the good opinion of the father if the course of wooing is to run smoothly.'

'In which case, give them to Mum,' I say. 'She loves flowers.'

Mum appears behind me. 'Hello, Jack! Don't stand out there in the cold. Why haven't you asked him in, Lily?'

I step aside to let Jack pass. 'He's brought you some flowers,' I say maliciously.

'How thoughtful! I'll fetch a vase.' She disappears towards the kitchen.

Jack's eyes are alight with laughter. 'You don't plan to make this easy for me, do you?'

'You're having a little too much fun with this. It's time I did too.'

I inspect the flowers more closely. 'These aren't lilies. Everyone brings me lilies. They seem to think it's funny.'

'They're daisies,' he says. 'Your favourite flower. You were misnamed.'

'I've often thought that,' I agree. 'Although if my parents had named me Daisy, my favourite flowers would probably have been lilies.'

Mum comes back with the vase. 'Let me put these in some water.'

I relent towards Jack. It was thoughtful of him to remember my favourite flowers. 'Actually, I think they're for me.'

Mum smiles. 'I'd already guessed that. You mustn't mind Lily teasing you, Jack. She does it to us all.'

She bustles off towards the kitchen with the daisies.

Jack laughs. 'She has the measure of you.'

I'm surprised. I've always thought my sarcasm bounced off Mum unnoticed. It's unsettling to think she may have been less oblivious than I realised and just decided to let it pass.

'We should get going,' I say.

Jack looks disappointed. 'What – no interrogation from your father? No instructions as to the only proper way to treat his daughter?'

'If anything, they believe you're doing me a favour.'

'Don't give me that,' he says. 'They think the sun shines out of you and Ben. Neither of you can do anything wrong.'

I reach for my coat. 'So, now you're telling me I'm a spoiled brat?'

'Oddly enough, I'm not. Quite the opposite, in fact. You and Ben have turned out fine despite it all – or because of it.'

'We're very lucky to have such great parents,' I say, following him to the door. 'Although I personally think they're batting one for two. I turned out great. Ben, not so much.'

Mum reappears, holding the vase of daisies. 'I'll take these up to your bedroom, Lily. You can see them before you go to sleep, and they'll be the first thing you see when you wake up in the morning, so you can think of Jack.'

As soon as we're out on the drive, I mime throwing up.

Jack waits patiently until I've finished. 'I'm hurt. This early in our relationship, we should be thinking of each other all the time.'

He opens my car door, and I climb inside. A horrible thought strikes me. I wait until we're driving out of the village before voicing it.

'I was thinking about what my mum said about putting the flowers in my bedroom so I can think of you. You don't think they'll expect us to spend the night together at some point?'

'No idea,' he says. 'Do your boyfriends usually sleep over at your parents' house?'

'Oh yes!' I say airily. 'At one point, I considered asking Dad to put in a revolving bedroom door to make things easier.'

'I wasn't trying to be offensive,' he says.

'I didn't think you were. Stephen is the only one who's ever stayed over, and it was pretty awkward. Everyone was so hideously polite and unconcerned. I tried to avoid it after that.'

'There you are,' he says. 'Your parents won't want you to be uncomfortable.'

'But you have your own place. Will they expect me to stay over there?'

'No one expects anything,' he says a little shortly. 'Your life is your own concern, Lily. You know that. There's a junction coming up. Which way do I turn?'

I direct him towards Banford, wondering at what point he'll realise where we're headed. Hopefully, not for a while. I'd like to surprise him. He's amazing at selecting thoughtful and unusual gifts, and it's my turn to reciprocate.

We chat about nothing in particular as we drive through the forest. I glance at him when we're three minutes away from the restaurant. He doesn't look excited, although he must have twigged where we're going.

'Left at that junction,' I say, pointing. 'Then take the second left and we're there.'

He slows down as we reach the end of the long driveway that leads to The Oasis. 'Now where?'

'Down there! Didn't you realise where I was taking you?'

He noses the car down the driveway. 'This is where we're going?'

I grin at him. 'Surprise!'

He pulls up outside the restaurant and turns to look at me. 'You can't be serious?'

'Perfectly. You told me you wanted to eat here. Don't say you've changed your mind?'

He seems dazed. 'Not at all, but I'm still not sure you're serious. When we started heading in this direction about ten minutes ago, I thought it was an elaborate joke. I suspected you'd discovered a fast-food place in the vicinity and were taking me there instead.'

'That would be a horrible thing to do,' I say. 'You don't really think I'd do that?'

'Not really,' he says. 'But how … I mean, how is it possible …?'

'Isabella got us the table.'

'Isabella?' he says. 'Horsey, unpleasant Isabella? The Isabella who stole your ex-boyfriend?'

I wish I hadn't expressed my opinions quite so freely, especially about someone I'd never met.

'I've got to know her a bit this week,' I say with as much dignity as I can muster. 'She's quite nice. I told her you wanted to come here, and she said her family knows the head chef and she could get us a table. The details don't matter. The important thing is that we're eating here. I hope it's everything you dreamed of.'

Before I realise what he's doing, he leans over and kisses my cheek. 'Thank you, Lily. You're the best.'

I mumble something in reply. Jack isn't usually so demonstrative. He always hugs me when he sees me, but I'm not sure he's ever kissed me. Not that this was an actual kiss, at least not a boyfriendly kiss. Then again, he isn't my boyfriend, so that makes sense.

'Our table is booked for eight o'clock,' I say awkwardly. 'We've arrived in good time. Let's go inside. There's plenty of time for you to buy me a birthday drink before dinner.'

Chapter Eighteen

I don't know what I expected when I walked into The Oasis, but it wasn't this. I thought there would be gold fittings and chandeliers and servers scurrying around in white jackets and bowties. Instead, this is low key and casual. At first, I'm not sure we've come to the right place.

A man wearing a trendy sports jacket and chinos comes over to greet us. 'Good evening, and welcome to The Oasis. May I have your name, please?'

'I booked it in your name,' I tell Jack.

He looks surprised. 'Jack Fisher,' he says. 'We were hoping to have a drink first.'

'The bar is over there,' says the man. 'Let me know when you're ready to be seated. May I take your coats?'

We walk over to the bar, where a young woman is polishing glasses.

'What's it to be?' asks Jack. 'Champagne? Or would you prefer a pint of Guinness?'

'Champagne sounds lovely, thank you.'

'It's my fiancée's birthday,' he tells the woman, who smiles.

'Happy birthday. I'm sure you'll enjoy your evening.'

She pours us both a glass of champagne and disappears.

'Why did you say it was my birthday?' I ask.

'I was under the impression it was.'

'But you know how much I hate strangers knowing that.'

'I do,' he agrees.

'So, why?'

'Why did you tell your mother those daisies were for her?' he counters.

I give a reluctant smile. 'Point taken. That makes us even. Actually, it doesn't. Why did you also tell her I was your fiancée?'

He gives me a soulful look. 'I may have been jumping the gun a little. I was planning to propose to you over dinner tonight, but now you've spoiled the surprise.'

My mouth falls open before I see his expression. I relax. 'Of course, you were. I shall inspect my desert carefully, so I don't break my teeth on the diamond ring.'

'Zirconium,' he corrects me.

I giggle. 'Can you imagine Mum's face if I came home with a ring on my finger?'

'I was worried she might be expecting it,' he says. 'Especially when she hears where I've brought you tonight. Why did you put the table in my name? You know women are allowed to go to restaurants on their own these days?'

'I'm aware. Isabella asked me which name I wanted to use for the reservation when she called, and I thought it was better to give her yours. There's a tiny chance she might mention it to Stephen, and it could get back to my mum. She'd be horrified if she thought you hadn't arranged this evening for me. You know how old-fashioned she is.'

He nods and raises his glass. 'What shall we drink to? Your birthday, but what else? True love and happily-ever-afters?'

I clink my glass against his. 'To friendship.'

He smiles. 'I'll drink to that.'

We finish our champagne, and the server shows us to our table. I stifle a giggle as he spreads the napkin in my lap for me.

Jack looks even more horrified when the server does the same for him.

'Do you think he's worried about our table manners?' I ask when the server has left.

'I expect it's because they serve lots of splashy food,' he says. 'It's probably their thing.'

He inspects the menu. 'You see? I was right. Consommé, turtle broth, mushroom tart.'

'Mushroom tart isn't runny,' I say.

'It might be the way they cook it,' he says. 'The only way to get a Michelin star is to have a unique selling point. This chef has probably gone for runniness.'

'Even the bread?' I say.

'I expect they dip it into some sort of liquid before serving it. Some exclusive brand of water that costs ten pounds a glass.'

'Which reminds me,' I say. 'This dinner is on me.'

'But it's your birthday!' he objects.

'As you insist on telling all and sundry. But you got the last one, and I want to get this one. I was excited to surprise you.'

He squeezes my hand. 'You certainly did that.'

I almost pull my hand away, then stop. It's a friendly gesture, like kissing me on the cheek. It isn't intimate to squeeze someone's hand in public, but it's the sort of gesture that would make Mum and Dad give each other a meaningful look and a knowing smile.

The server shows no sign of being overcome by the romance of it all. He's too busy greeting the couple who've just come in. He takes the woman's coat. As her hood falls back, the light catches her fair, curly hair. It can't be! But there's no mistaking the broad shoulders and dark wavy hair of the man she's with. What are they doing here?

'Is something wrong?' asks Jack.

His eyes follow mine, and his face assumes an impassive expression. 'I didn't realise you'd asked anyone to join us.'

'I haven't!' I say. 'I have no idea what they're doing here. Isabella didn't mention it when she called to tell me about the reservation.'

I lift my menu, trying to shield my face. 'Don't keep looking in their direction. They'll see us.'

Jack's face relaxes. 'Lily, there are eight tables, and the dining room is only fractionally larger than your parents' living room. Short of diving under the table, I think we'll be seen.'

I chance another look towards the doorway. As luck would have it, Stephen has turned to inspect the room. His eyes meet mine, and I stare at him, unable to move.

Isabella's face lights up when she sees me. 'You made it! I'm so glad. Are you having a lovely time?'

'Yes, thank you,' I say through stiff lips.

She gives Jack a tiny wave. 'Don't worry, we aren't here to gate crash your special evening. When I asked Uncle Henry if he could enquire about a table for two, he thought I said two tables. I was going to call and cancel, but then I remembered how lovely it was here. Stephen and I will sit on the other side of the room. You won't even know we're here.'

Stephen lays a hand on her shoulder. 'This isn't a good idea. You should have mentioned it to me beforehand.'

Her face falls. 'You're right. We should leave. We can get a table at The Wild Horse. I'll let Michael know we won't be staying.'

I breathe a sigh of relief. 'Sorry about that,' I begin.

Jack is quicker. He holds out his hand to Stephen. 'Nice to see you again. There's no need for you to leave. In fact, why don't you join us?'

Chapter Nineteen

I'm not sure which of us looks more horrified, Stephen or me. I give a strangled squeak, while he makes a sort of growling sound, which he turns into a cough.

'It's kind of you,' he says, 'but we wouldn't dream of it.'

'Nonsense,' says Jack. 'You and I have never had the chance to talk properly, Stephen, and this is a great opportunity to get to know Isabella.'

I glare at him. What does he think he's doing? It's bad enough that we've run into my old boyfriend with his new girlfriend without spending the entire evening with them. What happened to being British and pretending the other people don't exist?

Isabella looks doubtful. 'It could be fun, but it's Lily's birthday. It's a special night for you two. You don't want anyone gate crashing it.'

'Exactly!' says Stephen in a relieved tone.

I'm about to agree with him when I realise he thinks I can't bear to have anyone else around on my romantic date. He may even, heaven forbid, imagine Jack is planning to propose to me tonight. After all, I told him I was in an extremely serious, albeit surprisingly new, relationship.

He can't really think that. Jack would hardly have asked him and Isabella to join us if this was what he planned. On the other hand, some people invite an entire baseball stadium to witness their over-the-top proposals. Only inviting two onlookers seems quite modest by comparison.

'It's a great idea,' I say in an unconcerned tone, trying to look as though I don't care if the server pushes all eight of the dining tables together and covers them with a parachute before sitting down to eat with us.

'I knew you'd agree,' says Jack.

'If you're sure,' says Isabella. 'Maybe they can move us to a larger table.'

'We don't want to put them to so much trouble,' says Stephen, but in the tone of a man who knows he's lost.

I wonder whether his objection is to spending time with me, or whether he wanted to be alone with Isabella. He may have been looking forward to a lovely romantic evening of whispering sweet nothings into her ear. Jack's suggestion has put a spoke in that wheel, I think with satisfaction.

Isabella disappears to speak to the server, leaving the three of us staring at each other in silence.

Jack is the first to break it. 'Have you been here before?' he asks Stephen.

Stephen doesn't appear to be paying attention. I'd like to believe he's distracted by my beauty and rendered tongue-tied by bitter regrets about what he's carelessly thrown away, but he just looks annoyed. I recognise that look only too well from the odd evening we fell out, when he remained monosyllabic until I apologised.

I can't imagine Isabella apologising when she's done nothing wrong. Her mother will have taught her a hundred ways to deal with that sort of situation, most of them involving ordering a taxi and putting it on her date's account.

My mother would be more likely to advise me to smooth over troubled waters because she hates atmospheres and sees no need for them. She may be right. She and Dad have had a long and happy marriage. But I can't help hoping Isabella doesn't allow Stephen to get away with half the things I did.

Stephen seems to come back to reality with a start and realise he's being spoken to. 'This is the first time I've been here. Isabella assures me it's very nice. Good food, and all that.'

Jack seems to find this amusing. 'I believe it's been well reviewed.'

The server returns and directs us to a table near to the fireplace. 'I hope you find this table to your satisfaction.'

Stephen pulls out Isabella's chair for her, and Jack promptly does the same for me. I suppress an urge to giggle and give him a demure smile. The server brings our menus.

Isabella picks hers up. 'Have you decided what to order?'

'Not even close,' says Jack. 'We were busy arguing –' he catches my eye – 'I mean discussing whose turn it was to pay.'

'It's Lily's birthday,' says Stephen. 'Surely, you weren't expecting her to pay for her own birthday meal?'

'That's what I told her!' says Jack. 'But you know Lily, as stubborn as a mule.'

'I can't say I'd noticed,' says Stephen.

I give Jack a smug look. 'You see? Not everyone has such a low opinion of me as you do.'

'How can you say that when you know I consider you to be the pinnacle of perfection?'

He thinks for a moment, then adds, 'Darling.'

I can't give him a withering look in front of Isabella and Stephen, but once we're alone in the car, all bets are off.

'Sweet!' says Isabella. 'I'm still waiting for someone who thinks I'm perfect.'

I can't help asking, 'Doesn't Stephen?'

She laughs. 'He doesn't give any sign of it.'

Stephen flushes. 'This is a ridiculous conversation. No one's perfect. It's silly to pretend they are.'

'Don't tell Jack that,' says Isabella. 'It's nice to see someone so much in love.'

I catch Stephen's eye and look away. I have no idea what he's thinking, and I'm not about to ask. At least he doesn't find Isabella perfect. He was clearly aware of most of my faults, but that never bothered me. It showed he loved me despite them. Unconditional love is rare to find, and that's what he gave me.

I didn't see any faults in him. I still don't. He must have some, but it's never been obvious to me what they are. The only fault I could ever discover in him was that he didn't want to be with me any longer. That wasn't even a fault, more of an unfortunate choice he may or may not regret. It's impossible to read Stephen when he doesn't want you to.

Isabella doesn't seem perturbed by the idea of her boyfriend not worshipping the ground she walks on. She appears to find the subject more fascinating than upsetting.

'Do you feel the same way about Jack?' she asks me. 'Do you think he's perfect, too?'

I give a snort of laughter. 'Not remotely!'

I grin at Jack, who gives me a saintly smile in return.

'Don't look like that,' I tell him. 'You have plenty of faults. And despite what you say, you know I do too.'

He laughs. 'Maybe a couple of very tiny ones, but they're vastly outweighed by the good points.'

'The same with you,' I say.

'This is all fascinating,' says Stephen, 'but we should order.'

'You're right,' I say. 'Everything looks so good that I want to try it all. Do you have any recommendations, Isabella?'

'They do a tasting plate,' she says. 'We could order that for the table.'

'Not for me, thanks,' says Stephen. 'I think I'll have the pheasant.'

I'd forgotten he isn't keen on sharing food. It's one of his foibles. I can hardly call it a fault. He was always happy for me to order anything I wanted, as long as I didn't eat off his plate.

'I'm quite keen to try the Beef Wellington,' says Isabella. 'Uncle Henry says it's the best he's ever tasted. You two could share the tasting menu,' she says to me.

The thought of sharing a host of dishes with Jack under Stephen's disapproving eye is too much to contemplate. It would give an air of intimacy I'm keen to avoid. Knowing Jack, he would insist on us nibbling a bread stick from opposite ends just to embarrass me.

'I'm having the venison,' I say. 'It looks fantastic.'

Jack is clearly aware of what has been going through my mind. 'Are you sure, Lily? It would be so romantic.'

'Perfectly sure,' I say. 'What are you having?'

'The trout,' he decides. 'I'll enjoy it in lonely splendour.'

Isabella opens the menu again. 'They do a wonderful chocolate soufflé for two, but you have to order it in advance. It takes about an hour.'

'Marvellous!' says Jack. 'Lily and I will have that. How about you and Stephen?'

'I never eat dessert,' says Stephen.

This is true. He's rigidly disciplined about his eating habits. He runs five miles each morning and goes to the gym three times a week. But this is a special occasion.

'Can't you make an exception for once?' I say. 'How often do you get to eat at a place like this?'

'Quite right,' says Isabella. 'Don't be such a stick in the mud, Stephen.'

He looks embarrassed. 'I'll order something after the meal if I have room.'

'Why don't you order the chocolate soufflé?' I suggest to Isabella. 'I bet you could finish it all by yourself. If not, Jack is sure to volunteer. I've never seen him refuse a dessert.'

'Quite right,' agrees Jack. 'It's a shame to let something delicious go to waste. Think of all the starving people at Weight Watchers.'

'I'll do that,' says Isabella. 'Stephen can have some if he likes, but I'll manage fine without him.'

Does she mean this literally or metaphorically? Hopefully, the latter. She's so sorted and independent, and Stephen has always struck me as the sort of man who needs someone to need him. I'm not getting that vibe off Isabella at all. This may be wishful thinking, but I hope not.

As soon as the server has taken our order, Isabella returns to the previous subject. She seems fascinated by this discussion of our failings. I can't think why.

'Lily, you were about to tell us about Jack's faults,' she says. 'I'm all ears.'

I look at Jack, who doesn't appear bothered.

'He's always late for everything,' I say with a sidelong glance at Stephen. I know how much he hates unpunctuality.

'I'm late for everything too!' exclaims Isabella. 'That isn't a fault! It's a quirk.'

'It's an annoying one,' says Stephen.

She doesn't take any notice. 'What else?'

'He finds almost everything funny,' I say.

'Again, not a fault,' she says. 'You'll have to do better than that, Lily.'

'And he's the untidiest man I've ever met,' I finish.

Isabella looks at Jack with interest. 'Were we separated at birth?'

'My mother's never mentioned it,' he says. 'But I suppose anything's possible.'

I watch them laughing and feel a twinge of annoyance. There's no reason for this. It's no surprise the pair of them get on well together. They seem similar in lots of ways. I wonder whether Jack finds her attractive. Too bad if he does. She's going out with Stephen.

'In the light of these terrible revelations, would you care to revise your statement about Lily having no faults?' she asks him.

I brace myself for I'm not sure what. Jack gives me an affectionate smile. 'Not at all. She's the closest thing to an angel that ever walked this earth.'

'Sweet!' says Isabella again.

'I realise you're saying that to be polite,' says Stephen. 'But are you honestly telling us there's nothing about Lily you'd change if you could?'

I feel an odd mixture of emotions. I don't want Jack to say anything negative about me to Stephen. But this is a great opportunity to find out why Stephen dumped me. If it was for some specific fault, it would be helpful to know so I could work on it.

Jack shakes his head. 'I stand by my original statement. Lily is pretty much perfect in every way. Any imperfections she has are a part of her. Wanting her to get rid of them would be wanting her to be an entirely different person. I'll stick with the one I have.'

Stephen doesn't look as touched by Jack's speech as I feel.

'That's all very well at the beginning of a relationship,' he says. 'Everyone starts with a rosy view of the other person. But as time goes on, it's important to be honest about the other person's faults, and your own. Otherwise, you're sticking your head in the sand.'

'Honesty is important in a relationship,' I say. 'But communication is equally important. How can anyone work on themselves and fix things if the other person doesn't communicate?'

The table has fallen silent, and I realise I may have given myself away. 'Hypothetically,' I add.

Stephen is looking at me with an expression I can't quite read.

Jack is the first to answer. 'Why would anyone fix themselves to please another person? If you aren't a good fit, it's best to accept it and move on. You're bound to find someone else who suits you.'

'Plenty more fish in the sea,' agrees Isabella.

She may be right, but I don't want another fish. I want the first one I caught, the one with whom I spent two years, and with whom I planned to spend the rest of my life. He's sitting across the table from me, almost within reach, possibly thinking the same thing about me. I'm desperate to send him some coded message only he and I can decipher, but my brain has frozen, and I can't think of anything. All I can do is stare at him helplessly, willing him to understand.

The silence is broken by the server carrying several silver domes. He seems to know by instinct which one belongs to each diner.

He smiles around at the four of us. 'Enjoy your meal!'

Chapter Twenty

It's a relief to have something to do instead of continuing this uncomfortable conversation. Even though I had lunch with Mum and Dad, I'm pretty hungry, and this food is a work of art. The presentation is simple but as beautiful to look at as it is to eat. I can see why this place has a Michelin star.

Contrary to Jack's earlier speculations, the meat isn't liquid, and neither are the potatoes and vegetables. There's a redcurrant reduction that could just about count, but that's all.

'This is amazing,' says Jack. 'I haven't tasted anything this good since Lily made me toast and jam on Christmas morning.'

'Did you come home for Christmas this year?' Stephen asks me.

'Yes, Mum would never have forgiven me if I hadn't.'

'I expect she'd have managed,' he says.

I lay down my knife and fork. 'What do you mean?'

He looked surprised. 'Nothing. But she can't expect to have you home every Christmas for the rest of your life.'

'I don't see why not. It's a special time of the year for her. She and Dad always made Christmas wonderful for us when we were small. I don't think it's much of a sacrifice for us to repay the favour.'

'But you can't do it forever,' he says. 'What happens if you meet someone who also wants to spend Christmas Day with their family?'

'There's nothing to stop them.'

He smiles. 'And what if you have children? Won't you all want to be together for Christmas Day?'

He turns to Jack. 'Where did you spend Christmas this year?'

I realised too late the trap into which Jack is about to fall. I give his ankle a vicious kick, but he's already answering.

'My parents rented a house in Cornwall. It worked out pretty well for us all. My sister was there with her husband and children, and one of my cousins came with her boyfriend, so we had a big family Christmas.'

'Christmas was ages ago,' I say in a futile effort to change the subject. 'We're closer to Easter now. What are you doing for Easter this year, Isabella?'

'Hang on a minute,' says Stephen with a puzzled frown. 'You said you came home for Christmas, Lily.'

'That's right. Anyway …'

'But Jack was in Cornwall,' he says. His frown deepens. 'How could Lily be making you toast and jam on Christmas morning? Cornwall is hours away.'

'To people deeply in love, time and space is but a concept …' begins Jack.

'Don't take any notice of him,' I tell Stephen. 'Jack didn't mean Christmas Day itself. When we realised we couldn't spend the holidays together, we had our own Christmas Day the previous week.'

'What a great idea!' says Isabella. 'You and I should do that next year, Stephen. You can never have too many Christmases.'

He doesn't look convinced. I change the subject before he can return to his bizarre calendar obsession.

'What did you do this Christmas, Isabella? Mum mentioned that Stephen went skiing. Did you go with him?'

She pulls a face. 'Perish the thought! All I want to do at Christmas is to stay warm. I can never understand why people voluntarily spend a week sliding down mountains, only to take a cable car back up.'

'I think it sounds fun,' I say.

Skiing isn't on my bucket list, but if Isabella doesn't like it, it's a great way to differentiate myself from her in Stephen's eyes. It will show him that if he fancies going again next year, I'd be happy to join him. Not on Christmas Day itself, though. I'd prefer to spend that with my family.

'Lily?' says Jack.

I drag my thoughts away from visions of gliding down snow-covered mountains with Stephen, our arms wrapped around each other. Can people ski like that? I've never skied, so I'm not entirely sure. Perhaps one of them could ski backwards?

'Yes?' I say.

'Isabella asked what you and I are doing for Valentine's Day,' he says.

'Nothing,' I say before realising it's a perfectly natural question. Jack and I are supposed to be deeply in love. Of course, we'll want to do something for Valentine's Day.

'She's joking,' he tells Isabella. 'Lily knows perfectly well I'm planning a romantic surprise for her. She's very excited.'

'I can't sleep,' I say.

'How about you?' Jack asks Stephen. 'Do you have anything exciting planned?'

'He'd better have!' says Isabella.

Stephen looks uncomfortable. 'I'm sure we'll find something appropriate for the occasion.'

I can't resist saying, 'You told me you'd come home specially to see your new girlfriend. That was pretty romantic of you. By the way, how's your dad doing?'

'Fine, thanks,' he says shortly.

'What did you and Stephen do when you were together?' Isabella asks me.

'Not much. I'm sure he'll be more thoughtful with you.'

I'm pleased to see him look annoyed. I haven't quite forgiven him for the database book. And that weekend away in the lakes doesn't count now that I know he was planning to break up with me.

The soufflés arrive, and Jack's eyes light up. 'My favourite! If I didn't love you so much, Lily, you wouldn't get any of this.'

I pick up my spoon. 'Likewise.'

I'm not sure how to eat the souffle. I've shared plenty of food with Jack in my time – greasy kebabs at three in the morning after a night out, pizza and ice cream after break ups. But that feels very different to sharing the same dessert with Stephen watching us.

Am I supposed to start at one end of the dish and Jack at the other and meet in the middle? Is the dessert a metaphor for a loving relationship? Even worse, are we supposed to feed each other? The thought makes me feel hot with embarrassment.

'I'll put my portion onto a plate,' I tell Jack.

'If you must,' he says, 'although you're ruining the mood. I'll watch very closely to make sure you don't take more than your share.'

Isabella is already halfway through her own soufflé.

'Are you sure you don't want any?' she asks Stephen. 'It's delicious.'

She offers him a spoonful, and he gives her a faintly revolted look. 'No, thank you. I've had more than enough to eat.'

She doesn't look perturbed. 'I've never understood how anyone can have had enough to eat when something like this is on offer. It takes up almost no room.'

He doesn't answer. Not the first time, I wonder what drew the two of them together. Isabella is pretty, and she's easy to spend time with, but somehow, I thought Stephen would be looking for more than that. What do I know? I thought he and I were happy together, and apparently we weren't.'

Isabella lays down her spoon and surveys her plate with satisfaction. 'I give up, but I managed three quarters of it. Would anyone like the rest?'

I shake my head regretfully. 'I couldn't eat another mouthful.'

Jack pulls the dish towards him. 'I, on the other hand, could eat several more of these.'

'Too bad they take an hour,' says Isabella. 'You'll know next time you come.'

'At these prices, I doubt there'll be a next time,' he says. 'Especially as it would be Lily's turn to pay, and she's notoriously mean.'

He knows full well I can't comment, but I add this to the list of things I plan to discuss with him on the way home.

We finish the meal with coffee and liqueurs.

'Only a small one for me,' says Jack. 'I have to drive Lily home, and her mother will never forgive me if we end up in a snowdrift or worse.'

Stephen looks at his watch. 'We should really get home, Isabella.'

She pushes back her chair. 'I think I'll go to the ladies before we leave.'

'I'll settle the bill,' he says.

'Half the bill,' I say.

He looks at me with some of the old warmth in his eyes. 'Not at all. Consider it my birthday gift to you.'

'That's kind of you,' says Jack before I can speak. 'But this happens to be my birthday gift to Lily. I'm afraid I must insist.'

I wait until Stephen has walked over to the desk before nudging Jack. 'What did you do that for? He offered to buy me dinner. What's wrong with that?'

'You aren't his girlfriend,' he says flatly.

'I'm not yours either.'

'I'm aware of that. But you seem to forget he has a girlfriend. She's the one he should be buying dinner for, not you.'

'It was simply a nice gesture from one old friend to another,' I say.

'Fine, let's leave it at that. Anyway, I'm buying your dinner. It's your birthday, and I'm your fake boyfriend, so you don't have any choice.'

He strides off towards the desk before I can answer.

When we get outside, I see Stephen's Mazda parked close to the entrance. My feet want to turn towards it. I want to climb in as I always did and have Stephen drive me home. This all feels so wrong. He shouldn't be here with Isabella. He should be here with me. And there were several times this evening when I was sure he felt the same.

We say good night and walk across the gravel towards Jack's car. Something makes me turn and look back, and my heart contracts with pain as I see Stephen and Isabella locked together in the light streaming out of the doorway. He's kissing her more passionately than I ever remember him kissing me, and she's responding with equal enthusiasm. So much for him feeling the same way I do.

Jack hasn't noticed them. I follow him to the car and, on a ridiculous impulse, grab his shoulders and spin him to face me.

Before he can speak, I pull him towards me and kiss him. He pulls away, but I press myself closer to him. His lips part. I don't know whether he's trying to say something or responding to my kiss, and I don't care. All I care about is that Stephen knows how completely over him I am.

Jack's arms go around me, which prevents me from turning to see whether Stephen and Isabella have noticed us. It feels surprisingly natural to kiss Jack. I've never imagined kissing him before, but it somehow feels exactly how I knew it would. The smell of him is so familiar, the woody cologne he's worn for as long as I can remember, mixed with the faint coconut smell of his shampoo. His lips are warm, and I can taste the Benedictine he ordered after dinner.

He lifts a hand to cup my face and pulls me closer. 'Lily,' he murmurs, his voice seeming to come from a long way away.

'Mmm?' I don't want to talk right now. I just want to keep on kissing him.

An engine roars, and we spring apart as the Mazda turns in a tight circle and sweeps past us, spraying us with gravel. It disappears into the night, and I stare after it, my mind in a whirl.

'Lily?' says Jack again.

I turn back to him, almost surprised to find he's still there. 'Yes?'

He looks down the drive at the retreating Mazda, then at me. He opens the car door. 'Nothing. Are you ready to go home?'

Chapter Twenty-One

We drive most of the way home in silence. I'm not sure what happened back there. I kissed Jack on a stupid impulse I now regret. The only reason I enjoyed it was that it showed Stephen how little I cared about seeing him kiss Isabella. I would never have done it if I'd had time to think.

I'm also puzzled by Stephen doing something like that where he must have known Jack and I would see him. He isn't one for public demonstrations of affection. He was uncomfortable even holding my hand in public.

Was the display for my benefit – an attempt to show he doesn't care I'm dating someone else? It's an enticing thought, but it doesn't stand up to scrutiny. He couldn't have faked that kind of passion. He seemed utterly lost in the moment, as did she.

I imagine he also saw me kissing Jack, and that wasn't real. But the fact remains that Isabella is his actual girlfriend, whereas Jack is my fake boyfriend. Stephen has no motivation to stay with her if he doesn't want to. He could have come to me at any point and asked for another chance, and I'm reasonably sure he knows I would have agreed.

The unpalatable fact is that he must feel something for Isabella, and I've spent the entire evening cherishing unfounded hopes. I assumed because they bickered, and she contradicted him, that their relationship must be rocky. But perhaps that's their thing. Stephen may prefer someone who stands up to him. He's such a strong, decided character. I always thought he wanted an easy-going girlfriend who didn't challenge him. It appears I was wrong.

I file this away for future reference, although it seems likely there will be no future for us. If I was more like Isabella, I might have been able to keep his interest. I don't pursue this line of thought. I may still be hopelessly in love with Stephen but pretending to be someone I'm not could never work.

The best I can hope for is that she's a diversion for him — someone he met when he was feeling directionless and at a loose end. Much against my wishes, I like her, but I can't believe she's the kind of person he'll stay with long term.

My more immediate problem is Jack. I need to explain without hurting his feelings that I only kissed him to annoy Stephen. I won't put it like that. It's hurtful and unnecessary. I'll tell him it was a necessary part of the ruse. He and I had shown no signs of physical attraction during a romantic birthday meal, and I didn't want to raise Stephen's suspicions. It's a plausible and not too unkind explanation for what Jack must see as pretty bizarre behaviour.

An unpleasant thought strikes me. Jack kissed me back, and not in the amused way which might have been expected from someone enjoying this ridiculous situation. He kissed me in a way I'd expect from someone in a genuine relationship. He may have been acting, but if so, he did an excellent job of it.

I also did an excellent job of pretending I was enjoying it, but that was different. I was a prey to a range of conflicting emotions that he wasn't. I was on edge after an evening watching the man I love choosing to be with someone else. To add insult to injury, he kissed her right in front of me. Is it any wonder I retaliated in kind?

Jack doesn't have that excuse. He isn't in love with an ex-girlfriend, and he isn't hoping against hope she will see the error of their ways and ask to try again. I sneak a look at him out of the side of my eye. His expression is as calm as ever as he concentrates on the road. He doesn't look upset or annoyed. Then again, he never does. But I can't shake the nagging suspicion that's taken root in my mind. If I'm right, this whole charade is the unkindest thing I could have done.

I have to let him know as kindly as possible that my feelings for him are those of a friend. I kissed him solely for Stephen's benefit, not for my own, and certainly not for his. Yet again, I regret the stupid impulse that led me to set off down this road. Would it have been so bad if Stephen thought I was single?

What's wrong with being single, anyway? It's better than jumping in and out of any old relationship through fear of being alone. If Stephen was having second thoughts about ending things with me, it would have made things far less complicated all around if he'd thought I was unattached. It's too late to say anything now without making myself look even more of a fool, but I resolve to be more sensible in the future. It's unlikely such a situation will arise again, but it's as well to be prepared.

In the meantime, I need to clear the air with Jack and make sure he realises the game he and I are playing is nothing more than that.

'Jack,' I begin.

He turns his head to look at me, the usual smile absent from his eyes.

'I owe you a huge apology,' I say.

'Why is that?' he asks.

I try to adopt a light tone. 'You know what I mean, or do all your friends lunge at you and kiss you without warning?'

'Not on a regular basis,' he says. I still can't tell what he's thinking or whether he's annoyed.

'I'm glad to hear it,' I say in a tone of mock severity.

'What are you saying, Lily?'

'I'm trying to apologise. I had no right to do that. The thing was …'

'I'm quite aware what the thing was.'

I flush. 'Yes, well, I wanted to make our relationship look more realistic.'

'Is that so?' he says. 'To whom?'

'To Stephen! Who else?'

'It could have been to any number of people.'

'I don't know what you mean. You know perfectly well I'm trying to show Stephen I'm fine.'

'I wasn't sure what you were doing,' he says. 'You could have been showing Isabella she was welcome to Stephen or proving to yourself you don't care. You could even have been trying to show me something.'

This is the perfect opportunity to clear the air once and for all. 'There's nothing I need to show you!' I say.

'That's good.'

He isn't making this easy for me. I try again. 'While we're on the subject, I should clarify that I don't … I could never … just in case you …'

He swings the car into our street and pulls up outside my parents' house. He switches off the engine. 'Lily, there may have been some misunderstanding between us.'

'I think there has,' I say guiltily. 'I'm sorry, Jack. I didn't mean things to end up like this.'

He doesn't seem to hear me. He takes my hand. My first impulse is to pull it away. I don't want to add to his pain or appear to give him encouragement.

He looks deep into my eyes with no glimmer of his usual smile. 'Lily, I already have a girlfriend. I thought you knew.'

I'm not sure how long the silence lasts before I break it. It feels like several minutes, but it may be only a couple of seconds. 'You do?'

'I'm sorry,' he says. 'I was certain I'd mentioned her to you.'

'I think I'd have remembered it.'

It's a relief to see the old smile on his face. 'Who knows? You're extremely forgetful.'

'Tell me all about her,' I say. 'What's her name? How long have you been together? Where does she live? What does she do?'

He grins. 'It might be quicker if I forwarded you her resume.'

'It might be quicker if you answered my questions,' I say.

He shrugs. 'Her name is Carolyn. We've been seeing each other for six months. She lives in Weymouth, and she's an accountant.'

'She isn't a local?'

His eyes crinkle. 'Is that a deal breaker, as far as you're concerned?'

'I wondered whether I knew her, that's all.'

'I doubt it,' he says.

'Where did you meet?'

He hesitates. 'At a work thing.'

'You said she's an accountant,' I say, confused. 'You work in forestry. How could you work together?'

'What is this, a BBC detective series?' he complains.

'It's a natural enough question.'

'I suppose it is. I don't mean we met at work. I should have said I was down there for a conference, and I met her one evening at the hotel bar.'

'So, she's an alcoholic!' I say.

He smiles. 'Naturally. After being friends with you for so long, I wanted to find someone who could hold their drink.'

'You mean someone who wouldn't jump you purely on the strength of one glass of champagne and a small brandy?'

His smile widens. 'Exactly so. Not that I have any deep-seated objection to someone jumping me, just…'

'… not me?' I finish for him.

I know it's ridiculous, but I can't help a slight feeling of hurt that our kiss this evening meant nothing to him. I'm being irrational. It's just difficult to discover the two most important men in my life are taken up with other women. It adds to my current feeling of loneliness and isolation.

'I didn't say that,' he says, squeezing my hand again.

He sees my expression. 'Don't look like that. You're absolutely gorgeous, and you know it.'

'Not as gorgeous as Isabella,' I say dolefully.

'You're just as pretty,' he says. 'But the pair of you are very different.'

I sigh. The biggest difference I can see between us, apart from her long legs, blonde curly hair, and self-confidence, is that she has Stephen, and I don't. But there's no point in going over all that again, especially with Jack, who's been so patient with me about this whole thing.

'When will I meet this Carolyn?' I say. 'Will she be visiting soon?'

'I'm not sure. She's pretty busy at work, and so am I.'

'What about Valentine's Day?' I persist. 'You must be planning to see each other then. It's your first Valentine's Day together.'

'It isn't that big of a deal,' he says. 'Besides, there will be plenty of other Valentine's days.'

'Not with that attitude,' I say. 'You ought to do something special. I know how it feels when your boyfriend doesn't make an effort.'

'I'll think about it,' he promises.

'I feel I owe you a double apology for tonight's shenanigans.'

He laughs. 'Is that what they were? I wasn't sure.'

'What would you call them?'

He considers. 'Tomfoolery, hijinks, skylarking, pranks ...'

'I suppose I should expect that from a man who refers to dating as wooing,' I say. 'Regardless, I'm so sorry. I would never have kissed you if I'd known you had a girlfriend. I hope you know that.'

'Of course, I do. That's why I told you about her. I didn't want things to go too far.'

'You were worried I had feelings for you?' I say, surprised.

'I wasn't sure,' he says. 'You seemed extremely enthusiastic about that kissing business.'

'So were you!' I say, stung. 'That's why we're having this conversation. I was worried you might have got the wrong idea and thought this was something more than it was.'

He lets go of my hand and switches on the engine. 'A comedy of errors all around. I'm glad we cleared up our mutual misunderstanding. Oh, I almost forgot.'

He reaches into the glove compartment and pulls out a small parcel. 'I meant to give you this earlier. Happy birthday, Lily!'

I take it from him but don't open it. I'm still dazed by the twists and turns this evening has taken.

'You don't have to open it now,' he says. 'You should go inside before your mother wonders what we're doing out here.'

He leans over and kisses my cheek. 'Thanks for an amazing evening. I still can't believe you arranged it for me.'

I smile. 'You're welcome. I'm sorry we ended up eating with Stephen and Isabella.'

'That's fine,' he says. 'It isn't as though you and I are an actual couple.'

Why does he keep saying that? It's as though he thinks I haven't yet got the message.

'Are you alright with carrying on with the pretence for another few days?' I ask. 'Or would your girlfriend be upset?'

'Not in the slightest. She isn't like that. I would never have agreed to this whole thing if I'd thought it would upset her.'

I give him a doubtful look. 'Fine, but the minute Stephen goes back to Manchester, you and I are breaking up.'

'I'll look forward to it,' he says. 'I'll go home now and start working on a script.'

I close the car door, and he drives away, leaving me standing there, wondering what just happened.

Chapter Twenty-Two

I don't sleep much when I finally get to bed. It's probably all the rich food I ate at The Oasis. I can't help thinking about Jack. Why didn't he tell me about his girlfriend sooner? If he'd mentioned her from the beginning, I would never have allowed him to go through with this stupid charade.

Knowing Jack, that's why he didn't mention it. He loves anything ridiculous, and few things are more ridiculous than what I asked him to do. I hope he hasn't been laughing at me behind my back. Of course, he hasn't. Jack laughs with people, never at them.

However, this whole situation is excruciatingly embarrassing, and most unfair on Jack's girlfriend. I know how much I'd have hated it if Stephen had agreed to such a ridiculous request while we were together.

I toss and turn until the early hours, when I fall into a light doze, punctuated with feverish dreams. I'm almost relieved when my alarm goes off. Thankfully, it's my usual gentle music. I've been careful to keep my phone on my person at all times since Ben thought it would be amusing for me to be woken by a chainsaw each morning.

Mum is even more chipper than usual when I arrive downstairs. 'Hello, darling. How does it feel to be thirty-one?'

'Pretty much the same as being thirty,' I say, rubbing my eyes and trying to locate the kettle. 'Only with slightly more of a headache.'

'Sit down, and I'll make you some coffee,' she says. 'Did you and Jack celebrate too enthusiastically last night?'

'What?' I say suspiciously.

'It's fine,' she says. 'If you can't drink a little too much on your birthday, when can you?'

I relax. For a moment there, I couldn't think what she meant.

She makes me a cup of coffee while I try to prepare myself for the day ahead. My work isn't taxing, but I need to maintain a cheerful appearance for the customers. Mr Mason won't be impressed if I turn up looking as though I haven't slept for a week.

'What pretty earrings you're wearing,' says Mum. 'I haven't seen them before.'

'Jack gave them to me for my birthday.'

'How sweet!' she says. 'I don't have my glasses. Are they pink, sparkly hearts?'

'Almost,' I say, lifting a hand and gently touching one of them. 'They're cupcakes.'

She looks disappointed. 'Hearts would have been more romantic.'

'He knows how important cupcakes are to me,' I say. 'I think they're lovely. Speaking of cakes, did you try the one I brought home from the bakery on Saturday?'

'Your father had a slice last night after dinner,' she says.

'That's good. What flavour was it?'

'I didn't think to ask him. He said it was very nice. Would you like some for breakfast?'

I give an involuntary shudder. 'Please, no! But Mr Mason is bound to ask whether I enjoyed it. He'll think I'm very ungrateful if I say I haven't even tried it.'

Mum reaches up to the top shelf. 'Let's have a look.'

We inspect the contents of the tin. The cake is a beige-pink colour and offers no clues as to its flavour.

'The icing is white, so it must be vanilla,' I say.

Mum scoops out a little of the icing. She licks her finger. 'I don't think it's vanilla.'

She picks up a teaspoon and scoops up some more. 'It's definitely not vanilla. I'm not sure what it is. Why don't you try it and see?'

I groan. I'm not at my best in the early morning. I can usually manage some toast, but I prefer to save my cake tasting sessions for later. Why isn't Ben here? He can eat anything, at any time.

I reach for a spoon. 'Pass me the tin.'

Two teaspoons later, I'm as baffled as Mum. 'It's definitely not vanilla, but I have no idea what it is.'

'Banana?' she suggests without conviction.

'I don't think so. Maybe it's white chocolate?'

'Why chocolate isn't usually tangy, is it?' she says. 'Is it cream cheese?'

'Definitely not! At least, I hope not. It has some sort of fruity taste, which you'd hope cream cheese wouldn't. Let's try the cake itself. That might give us a clue.'

Mum cuts us both a thin slice, and we dig in. I close my eyes as I chew, trying to imagine I'm at a wine tasting session. I wish I was.

'It's light-bodied, with a fruity bouquet, citrus top notes, and a nutty finish,' I pronounce at last.

Mum looks puzzled. 'Do you mean strawberry or lemon?'

I laugh. 'I don't know what I mean. I can rule out chocolate, coffee, and vanilla, but that's all. It could be anything.'

She takes another bite. 'It's quite a pleasant flavour. Perhaps he meant it to be a surprise.'

I put my plate in the sink. 'That's possible, but it isn't how bakeries usually operate. Customers expect us to know what our products taste like. Never mind. At least, I can tell him I've tried it.'

'Don't be late for work,' she says.

I skid to a halt outside the Sugarloaf as Mr Mason turns the corner. He looks pleased to see me. 'I'm glad you're here on time, Lily.'

'I'm always on time,' I say with a saintly smile.

'I suppose so.' He seems preoccupied as he opens the door.

'Thank you for the lovely birthday cake,' I say.

He looks at me as though he doesn't know what I'm talking about. 'Birthday cake? Ah, quite!'

I reach for my flowered tabard. 'Are you all right, Mr Mason?'

He gives me a harassed frown. 'As a matter of fact ...'

I look at him in alarm. He isn't really ill, is he?

'Can I get you anything?' I say. 'A cup of coffee or a –'

I almost said cake, but he doesn't appreciate jokes about the staff eating the stock.

He passes a hand over his brow. 'No, thank you, Lily. My wife is rather unwell today.'

'I'm sorry to hear that,' I say. 'Should you be here?'

'What choice do I have?' he says. 'The village depends on our presence. It would never do to close the bakery unexpectedly.'

'I could look after the shop,' I suggest.

'You?' he says. 'All by yourself?'

'Why not? There's nothing too complicated for me to remember.'

He peers over his spectacles at me, and I correct myself. 'What I mean is, you've trained me very well. I know how to open up in the morning and close in the evening. I can use the till, and I know how the ordering system works if we run out of anything. Honestly, Mr Mason, I'll be fine. I think you should go home and look after your wife. If you give me your phone number, I can call you if I have any questions.'

He visibly wavers. 'It's an enormous risk, but if you really feel able to cope.'

'More than able!' I almost push him towards the door. 'I promise nothing will go wrong. If I can't get you on the phone, I'll call my mother. She could be here in five minutes, and I know she'd love to help.'

His worried frown disappears. 'What a good idea. It's not that I don't trust you, Lily. You've been a most conscientious employee. But it's no use expecting an old head on young shoulders.'

'Of course not,' I say soothingly. I can't resist adding, 'Mum has an old head on old shoulders, at least middle-aged shoulders.'

He gives me a reproving look. 'Your mother is a wonderful woman.'

'She is,' I say. 'You can rest easy knowing she'll come straight here if I need her.'

After a little more fussing and insisting on showing me one more time how to process refunds on the till, he disappears. I haven't had to issue any refunds so far, but it could happen. It's entirely possible that Bernard's owner will return at some point, telling me Bernard has cut his tongue on a raspberry pip, and she expects us to pay the vet's bill. I wonder if she'd be prepared to take the balance in doughnuts and cream slices. We always have plenty of those left over.

I busy myself for the next ten minutes uncovering the trays of cakes and unpacking the pallets of bread the lorry delivered this morning. I'm tempted to rearrange the cakes more attractively, making the brighter ones visible in order catch the eye of hungry customers. I decide against it. Mr Mason has assured me many times that his system is honed by long experience in the bakery trade. It doesn't appear to be a system that brings him much profit, but that's his own business.

I can't help feeling excited at being left alone in charge of the bakery. It's hardly a hub of activity, but if any crisis arises, it will be up to me to deal with it. Whatever happens, I have no intention of calling Mum. Ben would never let me hear the last of it. Neither would Jack, and I don't feel up to his merciless teasing right now.

I feel uncomfortable thinking about him at all. Last night was an absolute disaster from start to finish. I was so excited at the thought of our evening together. I was delighted to surprise him and looking forward to the usual evening of jokes and easy conversation, born of our long and uncomplicated friendship.

None of that worked out as I planned. First, there was the unexpected arrival of Isabella and Stephen, followed by Jack's inexplicable decision to invite them to join us. It probably didn't seem a big deal to him. He and I weren't on a date. We were having dinner together as so many times before. And, as he said, he always likes meeting new people.

I, on the other hand, found it extraordinarily difficult. Sitting opposite Stephen in a nice restaurant brought back memories of all the evenings we'd spent together in happier times. I'm surprised Jack didn't realise how painful it would be for me. It isn't like him to be so insensitive. His mind must have been elsewhere. Maybe he was wishing he was there with Carolyn instead of me.

I expect he was. They're in the first flush of a new relationship, when all you can think about is the other person, and you're counting the minutes until you see them again. It's odd he hasn't mentioned her before. There's no reason for him to keep his relationship a secret. He never has before, and neither have I. We always discuss our new loves and give advice and condole with each other when things don't work out.

It's obvious now that he didn't discuss his girlfriend with me because he thought I was developing feelings for him, which is ridiculous. He must know I'm still in love with Stephen. But I can't think of any other reason for his reticence. Our conversation last night certainly showed he was worried I had a crush on him.

It's so strange that we both came to the same conclusion about each other based on one stupid kiss. It isn't as though either of us enjoyed it. At least, not much. I was so caught up in the emotion of seeing Stephen and Isabella that I barely had time to think about what I was doing.

As for Jack, it's natural for most men to go along with it when someone kisses them, assuming they aren't utterly repulsed by that person. I hope Jack isn't utterly repulsed by me. And he happens to be an extremely good kisser, so it made it easier for me to pretend. But that's all. I wouldn't have done it if he'd told me he wasn't single. So, in a way, this whole thing was entirely his fault.

Chapter Twenty-Three

The morning passes at a snail's pace. The excitement of pretending to be a prominent local business owner quickly passes off. It's started to rain in a half-hearted, miserable sort of way. I wish it would make up its mind. I'm not too keen on rain, but a good hard downpour would wash away the grimy piles of snow dotted along the pavements. Fresh snow is exciting and magical, but snow which has melted and refrozen several times and now sits in grubby heaps is depressing.

People drift in and out through the morning, and I serve them without catastrophe. I haven't decided whether to close at lunchtime. What if I slip and break my leg on the way home? They would be no one to run the bakery this afternoon. It might not mean much in terms of sales, but Mr Mason is relying on me. This business is his baby, and I've promised to look after it.

I'm beginning to understand why he always seems so harried and anxious. It must be difficult if you don't have someone to pick up the slack when things go wrong. It's a bit like a relationship, assuming it's a good one. You know that whatever happens, someone else has your back and will do whatever it takes to support you, just as you would for them.

Hopefully, Mr Mason feels he can rely on me not to do any real damage while he's gone. I hope his wife is all right. I'll let Mum know about her this evening. She's always good at chatting with people and finding out what they need.

I've just decided not to take the risk of leaving the bakery for lunch when the door opens. Somewhat to my surprise, Isabella walks in. The last time I saw her, she was ... but I've promised myself not to think about that. Still, I can't help feeling embarrassed at having to face her again so soon. I'm pleased she hasn't brought Stephen with her.

She doesn't appear to share my embarrassment. 'How's it going? You're about to close, aren't you? I thought I'd stop by and see whether you'd like to have lunch.'

'I can't,' I say. 'Mr Mason had to go home, and he left me in charge.'

Her eyebrows rise in fake astonishment. 'You've been promoted to assistant manager already?'

'Hardly! It's only for today, and you wouldn't believe how difficult it was to convince him he wouldn't come in tomorrow to find the place a heap of smouldering ruins.'

'How exciting!' she says. 'Can I light the match? I've always fancied myself as an arsonist.'

'Don't even joke about it! It would break the poor man's heart. He loves this place. It's been his life's work.'

'I can understand that,' she says. 'But if he isn't here, you can take a full hour.'

This thought had already occurred to me, but I dismissed it at once. Mum always tells me that ethics are what you do when no one is there to see you. I've taken on this job, and I'll see it through to the bitter end – no shirking, no bending of the rules.

'I've decided not to close for lunch,' I say. 'I know it sounds silly, but I'm worried something might prevent me from coming back. I'll feel happier if I don't take any unnecessary risks.'

'Fine, I'll stay here,' she says. 'You can take your lunch break without leaving the premises.'

'I wasn't planning on taking a lunch break at all,' I say. 'As you can see, I'm not exactly rushed off my feet working here.'

She turns the sign on the door from *Open* to *Closed* and takes off her coat. 'Everyone needs a lunch break.'

She looks at our displays. 'What shall we have?'

'I'm not allowed to eat the products,' I remind her, but she waves a dismissive hand.

'That's a ridiculous rule. He won't miss a cake or two.'

'It will be a lot more than that if you're here,' I say, pulling out my purse. 'Mr Mason will return to find half the stock gone.'

She picks up a tray of brownies and inspects them. 'I have a healthy appetite, that's all.'

'So does a boa constrictor,' I say. 'Choose what you want, but I'm paying for it. You bought lunch last time, remember?'

'Fine,' she says. 'But I always tell Stephen I'm not a cheap date.'

She wanders over to the cabinet at the far end of the counter. 'I didn't notice these last time I was here. Are they meat pies?'

'So we claim. I've never tried one, but the customers seem to enjoy them. Go ahead.'

'I'll have the steak and mushroom,' she says. 'How about you?'

'I'll try the chicken and leek,' I say, reaching for the tongs. 'I don't know where we can eat these. There aren't any chairs in here.'

I pay for the pies and point her towards Mr Mason's office, which is the only available space to sit.

'Don't get crumbs anywhere,' I warn her. 'I don't want him to know we were in here.'

'I'll eat quickly,' she says. 'I've always found that's the best way to avoid crumbs.'

I watch in awe as she disposes of the pie in three large bites. 'How do you stay so thin?'

She laughs. 'Genetics, I think. My mum says I have a tapeworm.'

'Do you?'

She carefully folds the paper bag. 'I have no idea. I don't think anyone's ever checked.'

I finish my own pie more slowly, trying not to drop any crumbs. 'And what would your tapeworm like for dessert?'

She chooses a large eclair and a couple of my carefully arranged macarons. I'll have to arrange them into a new pattern this afternoon.

I select a chocolate chip cookie and lean against the counter to eat it.

'Is that all you want?' she asks.

'We don't all have your expandable stomach.'

'True, but if I only had room for one thing, it wouldn't be a boring cookie.'

I stop with the cookie halfway to my mouth. So much has happened this week that I'd forgotten about Stephen and the original reason he came to the bakery.

'Cookies aren't boring,' I say. 'We sell lots of lovely flavours. I'm sure you'd enjoy them.'

She crams both the macarons into her mouth at once. 'Cookies are what you choose when there's nothing else more exciting on offer.'

'I don't agree,' I say. 'Cookies aren't the most exciting product, but I love them. They're reliable and consistent and comforting.'

She takes a huge bite of her eclair. 'Is that what you're looking for in your baked goods? I'm not. I like new flavours and unexpected tastes, and I always enjoy trying things I haven't come across before.'

'In which case, you'd probably enjoy my birthday cake,' I say in sudden recollection. 'Mum and I had some this morning, and we couldn't decide what flavour it was.'

Her eyes light up. 'It sounds amazing! I'd love to try it if you can spare me a slice.'

'You can have as much as you like,' I say. 'It's the cake Mr Mason gave me. Mum made my usual coffee and walnut cake.'

She finishes her eclair. 'What do you mean, your usual? Do you have the same birthday cake every single year?'

'Of course. Doesn't everybody?'

She looks horrified. 'I doubt it. Don't you ever want to try something different?'

'Not really. I did as a child, but by the time I was about ten, I realised I liked Mum's coffee and walnut cake best.'

'You and I are very different,' she says.

I'm not sure how to take this. Of course, we are. No two people are alike. Is she making a point about Stephen? I scrutinise her face, but she shows no sign of hostility.

'I suppose we are,' I say. 'Are you using our baked goods preferences as a metaphor for life?'

'Not really,' she says. 'But I wish I'd thought of it. My uncle made me go on an incredibly boring course when I started working for him. We had to do this weird personality test. Everyone took it, but the questions were ridiculous. I didn't fancy being pigeonholed by some paper pusher, so I didn't answer any of them honestly.'

'I had to do one of those when I started my last job,' I say. 'It didn't occur to me to be anything less than honest. Your way sounds more fun.'

She grins. 'I filled in all the questions as though I was a serial killer. I wanted to see what results I'd get.'

I give a snort of laughter. 'Did it warn your manager you were a psychopath?'

'Unfortunately, not,' she says. 'I'd have loved to see my uncle's face when he got my assessment. It said I was focused and results-oriented and showed meticulous attention to detail.'

'The test sounds pretty accurate to me,' I say. 'Those results are exactly what you'd expect from a serial killer. They'd have to be all those things if they wanted to be successful in their chosen career.'

'You make an excellent point,' she says. 'Maybe there's something in these tests after all. What did yours say?'

'Nothing very exciting, as far as I remember. It said I was conscientious and liked routine and was prone to worry about my mistakes.'

'All of which is pretty obvious from meeting you,' she says. 'I could have saved them loads of money if they'd asked me first.'

'Is that what you thought of me when we first met?' I ask.

'Among other things,' she says. 'You were anxious not to overstay your half hour for lunch, which shows you're conscientious. And you'd managed to work in this bakery for a week without chewing your own arm off with boredom, which shows you like routine.'

'That makes me sound dull,' I say.

'I don't think so. It's only a tiny part of who you are. The rest of it can't be measured with their stupid tests.'

She considers me carefully. 'You're very kind. You look after that old fusspot you work with, whereas he'd drive me mad in a day. You have a great sense of humour, and you're obviously intelligent or you wouldn't have passed all those exams. I'm sure there's more, but I don't know you very well yet.'

I'm rather touched by this. She seems sincere.

'What about you?' I say. 'What would the test have said about you if you weren't pretending to be Hannibal Lecter?'

'Goodness knows! I don't really care. I'm comfortable with who I am, which is all that matters.'

'You always seem so confident,' I say. 'It must be nice to feel that way. I rarely do.'

'You should,' she says. 'You have a lot going for you. Look at you – good qualifications, lovely family, fantastic boyfriend …'

I turn away so she doesn't see my expression. I'd forgotten about Jack. At least, I'd forgotten he was supposed to be my boyfriend. Ever since I heard about Carolyn, I've tried not to think about him at all. Each new person added to this deception makes me feel more guilty. And Carolyn is now a part of it, even if she doesn't know it.

Isabella doesn't deserve to be a part of it either. She's been nothing but nice to me since we met.

'I'm very lucky,' I mumble. 'But you have a good job too, and your family sounds nice. And you also have a fantastic boyfriend.'

'True,' she says, but she doesn't sound convinced. 'That's actually what I wanted to talk to you about today.'

'Your family?'

'I'm talking about Stephen.'

He's the last person I expected to be discussing today. I can't read her face, and my heart contracts in fear. Has she realised I'm still in love with him and come to warn me off? I don't think I can face any more humiliation, not until I've processed what happened between me and Jack last night.

'Stephen?' I say in a strangled voice.

'That's the one,' she says. 'Do you mind?'

I shake my head. If she has something to say, she may as well say it and get it over with. It won't make it any better to wait.

Her face is uncharacteristically serious. 'I hope you don't think it's cheeky of me to discuss him with his ex-girlfriend. It wouldn't have occurred to me if I hadn't seen how happy you are with Jack.'

I'm tempted to give a hollow laugh but restrain myself. If only she knew.

'Is anything wrong?' I ask.

'I'm not quite sure. Stephen's a great guy, and we get on really well. But I'm starting to wonder –'

She breaks off and stares out the window. 'He's very attractive, isn't he? I mean physically. That's the first thing I noticed about him.'

'He is,' I say cautiously.

She smiles. 'I have no complaints about that side of our relationship.'

'I know. I saw you both last night.'

She raises an eyebrow. 'There's the pot calling the kettle black! We saw you too.'

I can't help feeling pleased my plan worked. So, that was why Stephen drove off so quickly.

'You know how it is,' I say, trying to sound casual.

'I do, indeed. As I say, Stephen is a very attractive man. But I've been wondering lately how well suited we are. I haven't thought about it much because it's early days. But then we had dinner with you and Jack last night ...'

'And?' I prompt her, hoping she says that seeing me and Stephen together made her realise that he and I are far better suited than they are.

'I was watching the pair of you,' she goes on. 'You looked so comfortable together. You practically finish each other's sentences, and you laugh at all the same things. Stephen and I don't laugh much. I do, but he doesn't. Last night made me question things more seriously. I want what you and Jack have, and I'm not sure I'll find that with Stephen.'

I have no idea what to say. I thought the pair of them were madly in love. They gave a good impression of it last night, at least the end of the night. I wonder how I can find out what Stephen thinks about their relationship.

'Have you talked to him about this?' I say.

'Not really. It's a casual thing. We've only been together a few months, and we don't see each other very often. Some relationships are worth working on, like yours and Jack's. I'm not sure this is one of them.'

I don't know why she's talking to me like this. It isn't, as I feared, because she thinks I'm after Stephen. In which case, what does she want? Does she want me to talk her into giving it some more time? That's the last thing I want to do. But I no longer want to break them up by any means possible.

'You told me you wanted some advice,' I say. 'About what, exactly?'

'About the best way to break up with him,' she says. 'You know him a lot better than I do, Lily. I don't want to hurt him more than I need to. I thought you might have some idea of how to do it gently.'

I stare at her, dumbfounded. Is the love of my life's current girlfriend seriously asking me how to go about breaking up with him?

'You know he's the one who broke up with me?' I say.

'I didn't. He hasn't talked much about you and him, and it wasn't my business to ask. Have I upset you? I didn't mean to.'

'You haven't upset me,' I say, surprised to find this is true. This is a bizarre situation, but I feel oddly detached from it all.

'I have to say I'm surprised,' she says. 'It never occurred to me that you hadn't broken up with him.'

'Why is that?' I ask with a painful jolt as I remember the events of a year ago.

'Because I've seen you with Jack. He's the complete opposite of Stephen. You and Jack have such an amazing relationship. I assumed you must have realised Stephen would never make you happy and broken up with him.'

A bewildering variety of emotions is sweeping through me. I can't untangle them, particularly not with Isabella standing right here. How can I tell her that Stephen is the perfect man for me in every possible way, and Jack and I are completely unsuited for each other? It's impossible without admitting I've been lying to everyone all week.

She seems convinced Jack is my soulmate, so she would take a fair bit of convincing. The only way would be to tell her about Carolyn. For some reason, I can't bear to do that, not until I've come to terms with having made such a complete fool of myself with Jack.

I need time on my own to get my thoughts in order and decide what I ought to do.

'I should open the bakery again,' I tell her. 'Can we talk about this later?'

'No problem,' she says. 'I have to go into work this afternoon, but I finish at five. Shall I come back at closing time? Maybe we can go for a drink.'

Going for a drink with Isabella is the last thing I want to do, but I can text her some excuse.

'I look forward to it,' I say untruthfully, wondering what Mum would say about my ethics if she could hear me now.

Isabella switches the sign on the door back to *Open* and waves goodbye. I watch her walk down the street and wonder what I'll say to her the next time we meet. It seems to be in my power to break up Stephen's new relationship, which is not at all what I expected when I met him last week. The only issue left to decide is exactly how and when.

Chapter Twenty-Four

Jack calls as I'm closing the bakery. 'How's it going?' he asks.

'Not too bad,' I say in a guarded tone.

'Do you fancy meeting up tonight?'

I was hoping to avoid him until I'd come to terms with the crashing fool I made of myself last night. But seeing him would give me the perfect excuse not to talk to Isabella tonight. I decide she's the more pressing of my two problems, and therefore the one I'd most like to avoid.

'I'm free around seven,' I say. 'I'm just closing up. Mr Mason left me in charge today.'

He whistles. 'Impressive stuff! I said you'd climb the greasy pole if you stuck to it.'

'How can I climb it if I'm stuck to it?'

'Don't be such a pedant,' he says. 'Are you up for a drink tonight? We could go to the Red Lion. That way, neither of us has to drive.'

If I have to face any kind of postmortem, I'm determined to do it with a drink in my hand. I'll use it to give myself some Dutch courage. If things get too bad, I can throw it in Jack's face and make a run for it. I'm not much of a drinker, but since coming home and embroiling myself in such a ridiculous set of circumstances, I've been thankful not to live in Prohibition times.

'Sounds good to me,' I say. 'See you there at seven?'

'I'll be there bang on time,' he says. 'Which probably means a quarter past.'

'I wouldn't expect anything less,' I say and ring off.

I finish closing up and call Mr Mason to ask how his wife is and reassure him nothing awful has happened to his shop. He doesn't answer, but I leave him a message telling him I'm happy to work alone tomorrow. After this, I text Isabella to tell her I'm not free tonight, after all, but I'll let her know when I am.

I arrive home feeling exhausted. Mum greets me at the door. 'You look pale. Is last night catching up with you?'

It is, but not in the way she means. I have the unpleasant sensation that several freight trains are rushing towards me at once, and I'm not sure which way to leap to avoid them all.

'I've had a busy day,' I say. 'Mr Mason's wife is ill, and he left me in charge of the shop.'

It's amusing to see the way her face struggles with conflicting expressions – sympathy for Mr Mason and pride that her little girl has managed the bakery all by herself.

Sympathy wins. 'That poor man! I'll pop around this evening and see if there's anything I can do.'

'Do you know what it is?' I ask.

'She has chronic bronchitis. January and February are always terrible months for her.'

'Poor thing,' I say. 'If you see Mr Mason tonight, let him know I'm happy to keep running the bakery for him.'

'Of course,' she says. 'Your dinner is almost ready, and then you should have a nice early night. You look exhausted. Did you have lots of customers?'

'The usual amount,' I say, 'but that's not why I'm tired. I didn't sleep well. I'm meeting Jack tonight, but I won't be home too late.'

She shakes her head indulgently. 'Oh, you young things. I can't keep up with you. Your father and I were the same at your age.'

I sincerely hope not. I'd like to think I'm the first one in our family to have messed things up to quite this extent.

Ben is absent for dinner. When I ask where he is, Mum looks delighted. 'Mia asked him over for dinner this evening. It's a good sign, don't you think? She wouldn't have asked him if she thought there was no hope for them.'

'It's a great sign,' I say. I really hope she and Ben manage to work it out. There's no point in us both being alone and miserable.

I reach the pub at seven o'clock. Jack can be as early or as late as he likes. I don't really mind. It's one of the things that makes him Jack. I remember he said to Isabella that he likes me because of my flaws, not despite them. That was such a sweet thing to say. I hope he meant it.

Somewhat to my surprise, he's already there when I arrive.

I join him at the bar. 'I assume your watch is broken?'

'This is me turning over a new leaf,' he says. 'I took on board what you said about my pathological lateness.'

'Don't say that!' I say, stricken. 'I was thinking that your lateness is one of your most endearing qualities.'

The corner of his mouth lifts. 'You're a difficult woman to please, Lily Carson. First, you tell me you don't like something about me. As soon as I change it, you ask me to change back.'

'I shouldn't have mentioned it at all,' I say. 'I felt backed into a corner, that's all. It would have looked strange if I'd said you were absolutely perfect. Stephen would have smelled a rat.'

'I see,' he says. 'What are you drinking?'

I wait until we're sitting at a table before asking, 'How does Carolyn feel about your lack of punctuality?'

'Carolyn?' he says vaguely. His brow clears. 'Sorry, I was miles away.'

He takes a reflective sip of his drink. 'I don't know. She's never mentioned it.'

'Which means it doesn't bother her,' I say. 'Are you going to tell me some more about her? I'm bursting with curiosity. All you've told me is that she lives in Weymouth, and you met at a bar. That wouldn't help me pick her out of a crowd.'

'What do you want to know?'

'Everything!' I say with as much enthusiasm as I can muster. 'How old is she? What does she look like? What does she like doing in her spare time? Can you see yourself staying with her forever?'

He lifts a hand. 'Slow down! This isn't a police interrogation.'

'Sorry.' I settle into my seat and wait for him to answer.

He takes a surprisingly long time to speak. He doesn't seem eager to talk about her. He may not want to jinx a promising new relationship by saying too much about it. Or he may be having doubts and doesn't want to discuss them.

'Jack, this is me,' I say when he doesn't break the silence. 'You can talk to me about anything. You know that. You've told me about your other girlfriends. Why not this one?'

'I don't mind talking about her,' he says. 'You just asked so many questions, I didn't know where to start. Let's see, she's a year or so younger than me. She's a similar height and colouring to you. She likes doing the same things I do. What was the last question? Oh, yes. Do I see myself staying with her forever?'

He downs the rest of his drink in one gulp. 'To be honest, Lily, I'm not sure. I'd like to think so, but I don't honestly feel it's likely.'

'Oh, well,' I say, sounding like Mum. 'Time will tell.'

'Indeed, it will,' he says with the flicker of a smile. 'What will be, will be. What goes around, comes around. We all have to go with the flow.'

'How wise you've grown since I last saw you,' I say. 'Seriously, Jack, I hope it works out for you if that's what you want.'

'It is what I want,' he says. 'But I have no idea what she wants.'

'Ask her! It seems the simplest answer.'

'Do you really think that?' he says, his expression unusually intense.

'Of course.'

I pick up our glasses. 'And now, I have something to tell you. I'll get us a refill first. This could take a while.'

I return with our drinks and sit down. 'I told you I was in charge today. Isabella dropped by to ask me to go to lunch, but I'd already decided not to close the bakery. So, she ended up having lunch with me at work.'

'Poor Mr Mason,' he comments.

'Mr Mason is fine,' I say. 'What the eye doesn't see, the heart doesn't grieve after.'

He grins. 'Aren't we full of platitudes today?'

'I think they're sayings.'

'Whatever,' he says. 'Get on with the story. What happened over lunch? Did the pair of you eat all the stock, so there was nothing left to sell this afternoon?'

'We tried,' I admit. 'But not that. You'll never guess what she told me?'

I lower my voice, although no one can hear. The pub is packed, as it always is on a winter's evening. There's far too much noise for anyone to listen in to anyone else's conversation.

'She told me she's thinking of breaking up with Stephen!' I lean back in my chair and watch his reaction to this bombshell.

'Is that right?' he says. 'I can't say I'm surprised.'

I jerk upright. 'I was! They were all over each other last night.'

'So were we,' he reminds me. 'And that meant nothing.'

'True, but we're in a very weird situation.'

'You're telling me,' he says.

'And I've already told you I would never have kissed you if I'd known you had a girlfriend. You know me better than that.'

'I do,' he says. 'I'm simply pointing out that one person kissing another isn't proof they're madly in love.'

'I don't see what else it can mean,' I say stubbornly.

He smiles. 'I don't suppose you do. You see things in black and white, don't you?'

'Another of the many things you love about me?'

He doesn't rise to the bait. 'I can think of plenty of reasons why a person would kiss someone in that way. They might feel they ought to, or they might want other people to see them, or they might be trying to breathe some life into a flagging relationship.'

'Which do you think was their reason?' I ask.

'The last one,' he says without hesitation. 'I've only just met them, but it was obvious within the first five minutes they didn't make sense as a couple. They're so different.'

'Opposites attract,' I say. I feel impelled to remind him of this because Stephen and I are opposites, yet we maintained a successful relationship for quite a while. Maybe we will again.

'Not that sort of opposite,' he says. 'Some differences are fine. An introvert can be happy with an extrovert, for example. But that isn't the sort of thing we're talking about.'

I'm surprised by his certainty. He barely knows Stephen, and he only met Isabella for the first time last night, and under rather unusual circumstances. It isn't like him to make snap judgements about anyone, let alone dismiss an entire relationship without ascertaining all the facts.

'What makes you so sure they aren't suited for each other?' I say.

I'm secretly hoping he says that, having observed me with Stephen, he can see us being very happy together.

'It's difficult to put into words,' he says. 'They have different outlooks on life. It's not that he's quiet, and she's bubbly, or he likes skiing, and she doesn't. It's more fundamental than that. They see things so differently, and they want different things out of life. A relationship like that never lasts.'

I'm pleased to think he expects Stephen to be free soon. If he is, what's to stop the pair of us trying again? I almost broach the subject, but it seems ghoulish to be picking over the bones of someone else's relationship with a view to making a move myself.

'What about you and Carolyn?' I say. 'Are you a case of opposites attracting, or are you one of those disgustingly over-compatible couples who wear matching sweaters and share an email address?'

'Never that!' he says with a horrified look. 'As for the rest of it, I'm not sure. All I know is we get on well, and we share the same values. Also, we laugh a lot.'

'That's a good one,' I agree. 'Although it isn't a complete deal breaker if everything else is right.'

'What did you tell Isabella?' he asks.

'About Stephen? I didn't say much at the time, but I texted her this afternoon to say it might be kinder not to break up with him right before Valentine's Day.'

'Is it any better to do it right after?' he says.

'I'm not sure. Neither option is great. Stephen broke up with me the week after Valentine's Day, and it was awful. It felt as though everything about that day had been fake. There was I, enjoying our lovely romantic trip, while he was secretly plotting to get rid of me straight afterwards.'

Jack's lips twitch. 'It all sounds very dramatic. It wasn't a murder mystery.'

His face lights up. 'Maybe it was. Is that why he took you up there – he thought it was a good place to hide a body? You had a narrow escape, Lily. I wonder why he changed his mind.'

'You aren't being very kind to someone who had their heart broken,' I complain.

'I'm sorry. I got carried away with the drama of it all. It was thoughtful of you to advise Isabella against doing that. You're a kind person, Lily.'

Speaking of being kind, would you like another drink?' I say, a little embarrassed by the sincerity in his voice.

He glances at his phone. 'I won't, thanks. I should get going. There are a couple of things I need to do.'

He helps me on with my coat, and I follow him to the door, wondering what these unspecified things are, and why he doesn't mention them. He probably wants to go home and call Carolyn. Of course, he does. It must be difficult to keep a long-distance relationship going, especially in the early days.

We step outside into the frosty night and start to walk down the high street together. A motorbike backfires behind us, and I swing around in alarm.

Jack takes my arm. 'It's fine. Just a motorbike.'

I don't answer. Even in the dark, I'm almost sure I recognised the couple going into the pub. The man had his arm around the woman's shoulders, and they were laughing together.

So, Isabella has taken my advice not to break up with Stephen right now. Was what she said to me today only a passing whim? Has she thought it over and decided Stephen's good points far outweigh the bad ones?

If so, where does that leave me? I gave up on Stephen entirely when I came home and heard about Isabella. Then we had dinner, and I wondered just how compatible they really were. But that was followed by seeing him kiss her, which confused me further.

I no longer know what to think. All I can hope is that things resolve themselves sooner rather than later. I can't take much more of this uncertainty.

Chapter Twenty-Five

I wake early on Valentine's Day and slip downstairs as quietly as possible to avoid Mum. I'm not in the mood for cheery conversation today. I pour myself a cup of coffee, pull on my coat and boots, and leave the house. I decide to walk the long way to work. I want to clear my head before I have to see Stephen and give him Isabella's cookies. It will be painful, but it may give me the closure I need and allow me to move on once and for all.

I thought Stephen was the love of my life, but it seems I was wrong. I fell madly in love with him and wanted to spend the rest of my life with him, but he didn't feel the same. When that happens, the only thing left to do is accept it with as much grace as possible and move on, hoping the heartbreak will gradually disappear. That's what I have to do now.

I walk several times around the village, warming up as I go. Yesterday's snowfall is white and unblemished, and the village looks like the illustration on a chocolate box. I walk past a row of thatched cottages and admire the way the snow has settled on the roofs, obliterating the thatch. They look like gingerbread houses with beautifully iced roofs, just like the cookies I iced yesterday evening before the bakery closed. The houses are far more symmetrical than my creations. Still, I did my best. As Mum always tells me, no one can do more than that.

Mr Mason arrives a minute after me and opens up the shop. We've fallen into a routine, which I find helpful today. I don't want to think about anything in too much detail. I want to get through the day, go home, and take a long, hot bath while I attempt to make plans for my immediate future.

'Did you put those cookies into a box for Mr Parker?' Mr Mason asks me.

'Over there,' I say. 'I expect he'll be in to collect them soon.'

He nods but looks distracted. 'I wonder whether you would mind looking after the shop for a couple of hours, Lily. My wife wasn't feeling too good this morning, and I'm a little concerned about her.'

'Of course,' I say. 'Take all the time you need. I can look after the bakery for the entire day if you like.'

He gives me a relieved smile. 'It's such a comfort having you here, my dear. I wouldn't have trusted the last girl to stay alone in the shop for even five minutes.'

Not for the first time, I wonder what this girl was like. Mr Mason has never been explicit, but from the occasional dark hints he's dropped, I picture her as somewhere between Typhoid Mary and Jack the Ripper.

'You should take your wife one of those,' I say, pointing to the heart-shaped cookies sitting on the counter. 'It's Valentine's Day, after all.'

'Do you know, I think I will?' He selects the largest one and puts it into a bag.

'Would you like me to ice a message on it?' I say.

He considers this. 'Perhaps her initials?'

I fill the icing bag with pink frosting. 'I'm afraid I don't know your wife's first name.'

'Daisy,' he says. 'Daisy Mason.'

'That's a pretty name,' I say. 'Daisies are my favourite flower.'

He looks pleased as he watches me pipe an uneven *DM* onto the cookie. I finish with a pink flourish and put it into a box, so the writing doesn't smudge.

He sets off up the street, clutching his striped bakery box as though it's the crown jewels. I hope his wife likes it. I hope the pair of them have a lovely Valentine's Day. Just because I've been dreading this day doesn't mean that other people shouldn't enjoy it. It's a celebration of love, and there isn't enough of that in the world.

I arrange the heart-shaped cookies more attractively on their tray and wait for the influx of loved-up customers. But either people have organised their Valentine's Day well in advance or Honeywell is one of the most unromantic villages in England, because an hour passes with no customers. I pass the time by rearranging the macarons into what, by narrowing my eyes and standing well back, might just about resemble a Cupid's heart.

I'm about to start taking inventory when a car pulls up outside. My heart contracts when I see it's Stephen. I take a deep breath and prepare to face him for what may be the last time.

He opens the bakery door and looks around. 'Good. You're alone.'

'Mr Mason's been called away.'

'I'm glad,' he says, coming up to the counter.

I reach for his box of cookies. 'Here they are. I've done my best with them. They haven't been iced to a professional standard, but you aren't paying professional prices.'

I try to smile as I hold out the box to him.

He doesn't take it. 'I came in to ask you to do me some more.'

He wants me to redo the cookies without even seeing them? I feel a flash of annoyance that he assumes my work isn't good enough.

He reads my expression. 'I'm sure they're lovely.'

'I wouldn't go that far,' I say. 'But it's a little offensive to assume I've messed up without looking at them.'

'I wouldn't dream of making such an assumption,' he says. 'I'm not managing this very well, am I?'

'Why do you need more? Do you have several more secret girlfriends hidden around the village I ought to know about?'

'No secret girlfriends,' he says, 'but I'd still like you to ice me one last batch of cookies.'

I reach for the icing bag again. 'I have no idea what you're talking about, but let's get on with it. I can't write a long message. We only have –' I quickly count the remaining cookies – 'six left. That's Isabella's fault for having such a long name.'

He smiles. 'I only need four.'

I select the most symmetrical cookies. 'Here I am, icing bag at the ready. What do you want them to say?'

'Can you write an *L* on the first one?' he says.

I obediently trace the letter *L* onto the first cookie. 'Now what?'

'The next one is *I*,' he says.

I squeeze the bag to make sure there aren't any bubbles and trace a wobbly *I* onto the cookie. 'I'm almost out of icing, but I should have enough for two more.'

'The third letter is also an *L*,' he says.

I obediently start to pipe another *L* onto the cookie, then stop. What's going on here? Four cookies, and the first three letters are *LIL* … There can't be that many four-letter words in the English language starting with L.

My mind races through the possibilities, but I can only come up with three – lilt, lilo, and lily.

There's no reason for Stephen to write the word lilt on a row of cookies. Maybe he's writing lilo because he's planning to take Isabella on a tropical vacation, and this is his way of telling her what to pack. I imagine them bobbing merrily on the waves on his-and-hers flotation devices, but I know I'm being ridiculous. Which only leaves …

I raise my eyes to his, hardly daring to believe what's happening. He's smiling down at me with the expression I remember so well, the expression he used to wear before he smashed my heart into a million pieces.

I can't speak, but my eyes ask a question.

He nods. 'The last letter is *Y*.'

I don't pick up the icing bag. 'But why, Stephen?'

'Because I've been a complete idiot,' he says. 'I threw away the best thing that ever happened to me, and I'm hoping it's not too late. Please say it isn't, Lily. I know you've been seeing this Jack guy, but that isn't serious.'

I stare at him, my heart pounding. I can't believe this is finally happening. I've hoped against hope all year that Stephen would change his mind and come back to me. And now he has, just as I dreamed he would.

Everything I've ever wanted is standing in front of me. All I have to do is reach out and take it. All I have to do is pick up the icing bag and ice that final *Y*, and everything will return to the way it used to be.

Stephen leans towards me. 'Lily?'

Even the way he says my name is the same it used to be – gentle, loving, and playful. A shiver goes down my spine as I remember he always said my name like that right before he kissed me.

I look down at the cookies, then at Stephen. This is all happening too fast. He isn't giving me time to think.

'Lily?' he says again. 'Perhaps I should tell you I broke up with Isabella last night.'

I don't want to say anything that might betray her confidence. But it's important for me to know the truth.

'Are you sure you broke up with her?' I say.

'What a ridiculous question. Of course, I'm sure. We had a long talk last night, and we agreed it was best for both of us.'

'She didn't break up with you?' I say.

'Oh, I see what you mean. No, I've been thinking about it for a while. We weren't as well suited as I first thought. Certainly, not as well suited as you and I were, and still are.'

He told me when we broke up that we weren't compatible on a long-term basis. But dating someone incompatible may have helped him to realise his mistake. I can't hold that against him forever. Everyone's allowed to make mistakes. I've made plenty in my time, one in particular since I arrived home last week.

'So, you've changed your mind about us being compatible?' I say.

'I'm so sorry, Lily. I don't know what I was thinking. It took me a while to realise the truth, but we got there in the end.'

'*You* got there in the end,' I correct him. 'I never thought we were incompatible.'

'Either way. The important thing is that we both realise how we feel. There's no mistake that can't be put right if we want it enough.'

'What about Isabella?' I say.

'What about her?'

'Was she devastated?' I already know the answer to this, but I'm interested to hear his take on it.

'She didn't say so,' he says.

'But you must know,' I insist. 'You broke up with her out of the blue. Surely, you'd expect her to be upset?'

He has the grace to turn pink, but he doesn't lose his composure. 'She may be sad in the short term, but she'll realise I acted for the best. If she and I aren't compatible, we shouldn't take it any further.'

'Is that what you told yourself when we broke up?'

He considers. 'I think so. It seemed unkind to continue with a relationship I wasn't sure about.'

He has a point. It's irrelevant that I didn't agree with his decision. No one owes anyone else a relationship. If one party decides it isn't what they want, they have a perfect right to say so.

'Are you going to check up on her?' I ask. 'Right before Valentine's Day is a pretty rough time to break up with someone.'

'I know,' he admits. 'I thought about waiting until after the day itself, but it seemed worse to spend the day with her, pretending everything was fine, and drop the bombshell straight afterwards.'

The conclusion he arrived at is the opposite of the advice I gave Isabella. But there are no absolute rights and wrongs in these situations. The important thing is that he thought about it and tried to do the right thing. It helps to restore my trust in him as the decent person I've always known him to be.

'I hope you check to see she's ok,' I say. 'Breakups are always difficult.'

I try not to speak in an accusing tone, but his face flickers. 'I know, and I'm sorry for how I treated you. That's one of the things I came to tell you today.'

'What was the other thing?' I ask. I know what it is, but I want to hear him say it. I've dreamed of having this conversation with him all year, and I refuse to be deprived of it.

He reaches for my hand. 'I wanted to tell you I still love you and ask if we can try again. I should never have let you go, Lily. I see that now. But it doesn't have to be too late.'

'You're aware I already have a boyfriend?' I say, moving my hand away.

He gives me a quizzical look. 'I'm aware that you say you have.'

'What's that supposed to mean? You've met Jack. You've had dinner with him, for goodness' sake. You saw us –'

I break off. That kiss wasn't my finest hour, and I've been trying to forget it ever since it happened.

'I know what I saw,' he says calmly. 'What I don't know is whether I was meant to see it.'

'Not at all! We were caught up in the moment.'

He doesn't look convinced. 'If you say so, but none of it rings true to me. Be honest with me, Lily. Are you and Jack really in a relationship?'

How dare he assume I would do anything so petty and ridiculous as faking a relationship to get back at him for dating someone else? It wasn't like that at all. At least, it was more complicated than that.

'You don't think someone like Jack could fall for someone like me?' I say.

'Quite the reverse. I don't think someone like you could fall for someone like him.'

I feel defensive on Jack's behalf. 'Why not? He's a great guy. He's smart and fun and easy to spend time with and –'

'I'm sure he is,' he says before I can enumerate any more of Jack's wonderful qualities. 'But that's not the point. You and he don't belong together. Anyone can see that.'

'Isabella couldn't! She told me we made a wonderful couple. In fact –' I break off. Stephen doesn't need to know it's one of the reasons she planned to break up with him.

'That's because she doesn't know you as well as I do,' he says.

His expression softens. 'Maybe no one does. I'm sure this Jack guy is everything you say he is. That doesn't mean the pair of you are romantically compatible.'

I want to argue further, but I remember Carolyn. There's no point in making a futile argument about me and Jack belonging together when I'm perfectly aware he's my fake boyfriend. Stephen has guessed the truth without much difficulty. I should have known he would.

But I'm not going down without a fight.

'You didn't think we were so well suited when we were together,' I say. 'It's only now I'm with someone else that you realise it.'

'No, it isn't,' he says. 'I've been thinking about it for some time. I almost contacted you in the autumn, but then I met Isabella, and I wondered whether I was wrong about you and me. She was so different to you in every way, and it was tempting to see whether she might suit me better. But I soon realised my mistake. No one has ever suited me as well as you, Lily. No one ever will.'

My heart gives a small flutter. That's a pretty romantic thing for anyone to say. And I know how much Stephen hates admitting he's been wrong. It must have taken courage for him to come here and admit it today.

There's still the small matter of Jack, but it will be a relief for him to hear Stephen and I are back together. We can stop playing this stupid game, and he can concentrate on his wonderful new relationship with Carolyn.

'I can't give you an answer right now,' I say. 'Whatever you may think about Jack, he's the person I've been seeing. He and I need to talk before I do anything else.'

The bell jangles, and there's a rush of icy air as the door opens. This had better not be Bernard's owner, here to complain he's thrown up the pineapple macaron she bought him yesterday, and she intends to bill us for the carpet cleaning.

But it isn't her, and neither is it Mr Mason, returning to his post. To my surprise, I see Jack standing in the doorway, holding a brightly wrapped parcel.

Chapter Twenty-Six

He closes the door and turns to face me. My brain is whirling too madly for me to speak. He looks at my flushed face, then down at the cookies lying on the counter.

'Lilo?' he says. 'Are you going on holiday, Stephen?'

I give a choke of laughter. 'That's what I said! At least, I thought it.'

Jack's mouth twitches. 'Of course, you did.'

'You're just the man we need,' says Stephen. 'Lily wants to talk to you.'

'Is that right?' says Jack. He turns to me. 'I think I can guess why. But go ahead.'

It's ridiculous to feel this surge of guilt. He'll be relieved to put this whole charade to bed once and for all. From the looks of it, he's heading off to visit Carolyn after this. I may as well tell him what's happening and get it over with.

'Stephen thinks you and I are only pretending to be a couple!' I blurt out.

I can't think what makes me begin with this. I meant to tell him calmly and quietly that Stephen has asked if we can give things another go. After long and mature consideration, that's

what I'm doing. After two minutes' consideration? Two seconds?
It isn't relevant. It's the right decision, so I don't need to spend
time agonising over it.

'And what do you think about that?' says Jack.

I don't know what he means. What does it matter what I
think? We both know Stephen is right. He's seen straight through
our ridiculous pretence. I don't know why I thought he wouldn't.
I'm lucky it didn't annoy him and stop him from asking me for
another chance.

'I'm not sure what you mean,' I say.

Jack doesn't drop his gaze from mine. 'I'm not interested in
what Stephen thinks about our relationship. I want to know what
you think about it.'

I draw him to one side, murmuring in a low voice so Stephen
can't hear.

'What are you doing? He's right. You and I have only been
pretending to have a relationship. We don't need to do that
anymore. Have you forgotten you have an actual girlfriend, as
well as a pretend one?'

'You mean Caitlin?' he says.

'You told me her name was Carolyn,' I say.

His eyes light with sudden laughter. 'Did I? That's because
it's the name her parents gave her when she was born. But when
she was five, she decided to change it because she didn't think it
suited her. Naturally, I call her by her preferred name.'

My mind is racing, trying to remember the conversations he
and I have had about this girlfriend. There haven't been many.
He didn't even mention her existence until the night we had
dinner at The Oasis.

What has he told me about her? They share the same values
and enjoy doing the same things, and they laugh a lot. What else?
She's a year younger than him and about my height and colouring.
He'd love to think they'll stay together, but he doesn't think it's
likely. That's strange in itself. If he likes her so much, and they
have so much in common and so much fun, why can't he see

himself staying with her long term? It must be because he thinks she doesn't feel the same way. There can't be any other explanation.

Jack is smiling at me in the way he always does when he isn't sure how I'll react.

Stephen clears his throat. 'Are you ready, Lily?'

I turn to face him. 'Why did you think Jack and I were pretending?'

'Is it important?' he asks.

'I need to know. I can't explain why, but it will give me closure.'

'Fine, although I don't see the point.'

He thinks for a moment. 'It's all pretty simple. I didn't question it when you first told me about your new boyfriend. Nothing was more natural than for you to have moved on. I was happy for you. But when I thought about it later, I wondered why you seemed so upset when I told you about Isabella.'

'You didn't just tell me about her. You asked me to ice her some cookies,' I remind him.

'True,' he agrees. 'It was an awkward situation all around. So, I put it out of my mind. But when we had dinner on Sunday evening, I knew for sure.'

'You did?' I rummage through my memory, trying to discover what gave us away.

He smiles. 'Come on, Lily. It's clear Jack isn't the right man for you. I started thinking back to our relationship and the sort of things we used to do together and the discussions we had about serious subjects. It was obvious you and Jack would never do any of those things. All you did was laugh and make jokes.'

'You mean we enjoyed ourselves?'

He shakes his head. 'That's fine as far as it goes. But I know you better than you know yourself, Lily. You're looking for more than that from a long-term relationship. You don't want to waste your time messing around with a lightweight.'

Jack starts to speak, but I lift a hand to stop him. 'Perhaps you know me as well as you say, Stephen, but maybe Jack does too.'

'As a friend,' says Stephen. His eyes soften. 'But he'll never know you as I know you. Which means he'll never love you as I do because he'll never understand the real you.'

The silence lengthens as I think about this. Is Stephen right to say he knows me better than I know myself? He's told me this me before, and I've accepted it as a sign that he and I are soul mates.

Jack is watching me intently, his face no longer amused.

'What's in the parcel?' I ask suddenly.

He looks down at the box he's holding as though he's not sure how it got there. 'Something I thought you might like.'

'Can I open it now?' I say, and he hands it to me.

I lay the parcel on the counter, smiling at the over-the-top wrapping paper, covered with silver cupids and bright pink hearts.

'Is this all they sell at the post office?' I ask.

His eyes dance. 'I had to go online to find that wrapping paper. It took me a while, I can tell you. Most of it was tasteful and discreet. But I got there in the end.'

I pull the paper away, trying not to tear it more than I have to. Inside is a vivid pink box. It looks familiar.

'Is this one of ours?' I ask.

Jack grins. 'I'm afraid so. I had to buy quite a few cookies before your boss would give me this. It took me a long time to paint it this tasteful shade of bubble-gum pink. But I knew you'd want something subtle.'

I inspect it more closely. 'The silver glitter is an especially classy touch. You used a fair bit of glue, I see.'

'The post office only sells one size,' he says. 'It seemed a waste not to use it all.'

I lift the lid and look inside. 'Cookies?'

'Valentine's cookies,' he corrects me.

'You realise I work in a bakery?'

'I do, but so what? It occurred to me that customers would be coming in all day to buy things for the people they love, and I wanted you to have something too.'

'Are these our cookies?' I ask.

'That's right. I wanted to do my bit to boost the local economy and make sure you kept your job.'

'It's hardly my dream job,' I object.

'But it's local,' he says.

I pick up the nearest cookie. 'What happened to this one? Did you ice it yourself?'

He frowns. 'This must be how Picasso felt when uneducated people commented on his paintings. It's a picture. Perhaps it isn't as sophisticated as your beautiful calligraphy, but I did my best.'

I peer at it more closely. 'Is that a wine glass?'

He looks pleased. 'Not just any wineglass. It's the one I gave you for your university graduation. It was Waterford Crystal, and it cost me a week's wages. You broke it a week later when we came home after an evening out and didn't dare put the lights on because of your grumpy landlord.'

'This one is even nicer,' I assure him.

I pick up the next cookie. 'Is this a mountain or a traffic cone?'

'It's a tent!' he says. 'Don't you remember that time we went camping and neither of us knew how to put up our tents? There was a thunderstorm during the night, and they collapsed on top of us.'

'And we had to take the overnight train home,' I say. 'Thank goodness the bar was open!'

He points to the next cookie. 'That's the train. I've smudged the windows a bit, but you get the general idea.'

I pick up the third one. 'Is this a snake? No, it's a rollercoaster!'

'That one took me a long time,' he says. 'The blobs of blue icing are us. I think I caught our likeness very well.'

'What's the pink blob?'

'It's the candyfloss you insisted on eating. I warned you, but you refused to listen.'

'I'm sorry I was sick on you,' I say. 'You didn't put that on a cookie too?'

'I'm not so heartless,' he says.

I look at the white shape on the next cookie. 'Is that an ice skate?'

'Got it in one! You insisted on taking me, much against my better judgement. You'll notice there's a bandage around the edge of the cookie.'

I turn to Stephen, laughing. 'I sprained my ankle really badly. We had to sit in Accident and Emergency half the night. All they had in the vending machines was cheese crackers and Dr Pepper.'

He doesn't smile. 'That sounds stressful.'

'It was one of the best nights of my life,' I assure him. 'I've never laughed so much.'

I look at the last two cookies. 'That multi-coloured one has to be trivial pursuit.'

'Drunken trivial pursuit,' says Jack. 'It's the best kind.'

I pick up the final cookie. 'I'm not sure what this is?'

Jack leans over to see. 'That's you wearing your new red dress, the one you wore to The Oasis.'

'And that must be you making a rare appearance in your smart grey suit,' I say. 'What are we doing?'

One corner of his mouth turns up. 'You're kissing me.'

'It looks more like you're kissing me,' I say.

'Does it matter? It's one of my very favourite memories with you. It belongs with the rest of them.'

I lay the cookie back in its box and turn to Stephen. 'I'm really sorry, but there's been some misunderstanding. I'm not sure why you think Jack and I aren't in a relationship, but I'm afraid you're wrong. He and I are in exactly the sort of relationship I've always wanted and never had.'

'Because he decorated a few cookies for you?' he says. 'You were about to say yes to me before Jack came in. I know you were.'

'Maybe I was, but it would have been the biggest mistake of my life. And it isn't because of the cookies. At least, not entirely, although they helped me see things more clearly.'

'This is ridiculous,' he says. 'You aren't over me any more than I'm over you.'

'Maybe I wasn't fully over you,' I say slowly. 'But the person I wasn't over was someone I never knew. And he didn't know me at all. Even when you came in here today, wanting to get back together, you expected me to ice my own name on those cookies. Jack took the time and trouble to do it himself, which shows he knows me better than you ever will.'

Stephen doesn't speak, and I feel a pang of guilt. I've never wanted to hurt him, and I still don't. But that doesn't mean I want to spend the rest of my life with him.

'If that's the way you feel,' he says at last, 'there's nothing more to be said. You have to do whatever's best for you, Lily. All I can do is wish you well.'

He nods to Jack and turns to leave the shop.

'Don't forget the cookies you ordered,' I say. 'You've already paid for them.'

'You keep them,' he says.

I watch him stride along the pavement and climb into his car. I can't believe what I've done. I've spent an entire year waiting and hoping for Stephen to come back to me. When he finally did, I sent him away again. I wonder for a moment whether I've done the right thing, but in my heart of hearts, I know I have. And I know exactly why.

I turn to face Jack. 'You've spent the past two weeks being my fake boyfriend, even while you thought I was in love with someone else. Do you think you could ever consider being my real boyfriend?'

He shakes his head. 'I'm not sure, Lily. This is awfully sudden. I need some time to process all these emotions and get some kind of – what did you call it – closure?'

I'm too disappointed to speak, so I just nod.

He grins. 'Sometimes, I think you don't know me at all.'

He takes a step towards me and brushes a finger over my cheek before tilting my face up to his.

'Lily, I've been in love with you for years. I've almost told you many times, but I was too afraid of losing you. Then you met Stephen, and I thought I'd lost you forever. I was going to tell you how I felt after you kissed me on your birthday, but then I realised you'd only done it to make Stephen jealous. It seemed that no matter what happened, you would always be in love with him, and there would be no chance for me.'

Tears are pricking the back of my eyes, but I'm too happy to cry. I look up into my best friend's face. 'So, what happens now?'

'This!' he says with decision and kisses me.

It feels like only five seconds later, but it could be five minutes, or five hours, when the doorbell jangles. I jump and try to pull away from Jack.

'Leave it,' he murmurs. 'Let the answerphone get it.'

'It's the shop bell. I'm supposed to be working.'

I turn around, expecting to see Mr Mason. He'll probably fire me on the spot for flagrant misconduct. At this moment, I don't much care, but it would be a shame for my career at the Sugarloaf to end this way.

It isn't Mr Mason. It's his arch enemy, the woman with the cavoodle. She's standing in the doorway, looking at us as though we've tried to force feed Bernard a chocolate brownie.

I smooth down my hair. 'Good morning. Can I help you?'

Bernard ambles in behind her and gives me an idiotic grin.

'I can't let your dog into the shop,' I say. 'My boss isn't here, but I know he wouldn't be pleased.'

'Is that so?' she says snidely. 'And I doubt he'd be pleased to hear his employee spends all her time canoodling while he's away.'

Jack looks delighted. 'Canoodling! I'll have to add that one to the list.'

'It's hardly all my time,' I tell the woman. 'And it's Valentine's Day,' I add in an attempt to soften her heart.

It doesn't have the required effect. She makes a harrumphing sound. 'That's no excuse. All this talk of health and safety, yet I walk in to find this sort of thing going on! I'll make very sure your boss hears of it when he gets back.'

I can't think of anything to say. Hopefully, I can persuade Mr Mason to take a lenient view of the situation, but he may take her complaint seriously.

Jack is quicker. He picks up Stephen's box of cookies and hands it to her with a courtly bow.

'In the spirit of St. Valentine, perhaps you would accept this as a complimentary gift for one of our bakery's most valued customers.'

She takes the box and peers inside as though she expects it to contain a hand grenade. She squints at the cookies. 'What do these say – I S A ...?'

'They're completely random letters,' Jack assures her. 'My girlfriend has made up several boxes of these. Any words or proper names you may form are entirely coincidental. But you can imagine what fun our customers will have with them.'

'Hmmm,' she says.

'I'm sure Bernard will enjoy them,' I add. 'He loves our cookies, and there's no chocolate in them.'

Bernard is yapping excitedly, leaping up and down to catch a glimpse of the contents of this mystery box.

The woman pats his head. 'In a moment, Bernie. Mummy will give you a lovely treat as soon as we get home.'

She tucks the box firmly under her arm. 'I'll let it go this time. But I don't wish to see this sort of behaviour when I come in here to buy my cakes.'

'It will never happen again,' I assure her.

'Don't count on it,' Jack mutters.

We watch the woman walk down the high street, with Bernard frisking around her in anticipation of the treat he's been promised. As soon as she's out of sight, Jack walks over to the shop door and switches the sign from *Open* to *Closed*.

'You can't do that!' I say. 'Mr Mason might lose valuable business.'

'I'll buy up his entire stock, if need be,' he promises. 'But I'm sick and tired of all these interruptions.'

I try to remember my staff training, the list of rules on the wall, my flowered tabard, and even the unflattering hairnet I now remember I'm still wearing. But it's no good. All I can think of is that I'm finally alone with the man who has loved me for years, patiently waiting for me to realise I love him too.

Jack pulls me into his arms, and this time I don't resist. The look on his face makes my heart pound.

'Happy Valentine's Day, Lily,' he says, bending his head towards mine.

I slip my arms around his neck and look deep into his eyes, a wave of happiness washing over me.

'Thank you for visiting us at The Sugarloaf Bakery today,' I whisper. 'I hope your experience was everything you hoped for.'

Thank you for reading!

If you would like to read an epilogue telling you what Lily and Isabella did next, go to this link to request your free copy.

rosemarywhittaker.com/a-new-start

A Sugarloaf Mix-Up

After meeting Lily and Isabella, Abby is delighted to land her dream job at The Sugarloaf Bakery. What she didn't expect was to set off on her own romantic adventure.

Join the fun in the second book of *The Sugarloaf Bakery* series.

A Sugarloaf Mix-Up is available now in paperback and Kindle e-book.

Books by Rosemary Whittaker
All available now in paperback and Kindle e-book

The Sugarloaf Bakery series

A Sugarloaf Valentine
A Sugarloaf Mix-Up
A Sugarloaf Surprise
A Sugarloaf Christmas
A Sugarloaf Easter
A Sugarloaf Secret
A Sugarloaf Summer

The Sugarloaf Bakery Books 1-3

The Christmas in Honeywell series

A Tale of Two Christmases
A Boxful of Christmas
The Christmas Cookie Club

The Year Away series

The Cinnamon Snail
Sunshine State
The Wattle Birds
The Feijoa Tree
The Villa Mimosa

A Year Away Books 1-4

Short Reads

Making the Effort

Made in the USA
Columbia, SC
19 January 2025

52104135R00113